Lock, Stock & Peril

A Novel

Dave McBride

Lock, Stock & Peril is a work of fiction. The story and characters are fictitious. Certain long-standing institutions and organizations are mentioned, but the characters involved and the occurrences at these places are wholly imaginary. The Thomas Edison of this narrative is entirely fictional. My imagined Edison does, however, abide by generally known facts of the real man's life. Descriptions of excerpts from Edison family letters are taken from correspondence curated by the Rutgers Edison Papers Project. Other names, characters, and incidents are either of the author's imagination or are used fictitiously and any resemblance to actual persons, living or dead, events, or locales is entirely coincidental.

Copyright © 2021 by Dave McBride

9 8 7 6 5 4 3 2 1 First Edition

ISBN 978-1-7365138-2-8
EAN 51248
ISBN 978-1-7365138-3-5 (ebook)
Library of Congress 2021906499

Cover design by Dave McBride. Photo of facsimile vintage Adlake #48 switch lock with permission of Adams & Westlake, Ltd. Elkhart, Indiana

www.davemcbride.com

To Anita, naturally.

Lock, Stock & Peril

Just because something doesn't do what you planned it to do doesn't mean it's useless.
—Thomas Edison

Chapter 1

Saturday

A breeze rustled through the papery seed pods awaiting launch from the fishfuddle tree, carrying in with it the slightest hint of baguettes baking. Sunlight spilled across the threshold of the open door. A mockingbird had recently acquired the block and was motoring through his setlist like a sprightly piccolo. Milo supposed that on such a splendid day, given the option, the guy under the sheet at the museum would have come down hard on the side of being alive to see it.

The clack and rattle of an empty Conch train rumbling over a patch of uneven pavement had diverted his attention momentarily from the annoyance who was his ex-boss. Milo returned the phone to the side of his head and his focus to the argument.

"It's only by unhappy accident we are having this conversation, Barry. I picked up by reflex. For months I've been counting down to the day I can set your caller ID on ignore. And that just zoomed to the top of my to-do list."

"Come on, don't be like that." Barry adjusted his tone to impersonate someone authentically offended by personal disrespect. In point of fact he was immune. "All I've done for you. I never doubted for a moment you'd be there when I needed you."

"No can do, Barry. I can't. I won't. I'm done." Milo shoulder-pinned the phone to his ear as he incised a carton with a box cutter. A shutter-sliced sunbeam cast bright lines across the package and the table like a radiant bar code.

"Please, Milo. You said you'd be okay with having my back if something big comes up. This is that."

Across the room the Eskimo held up a lamp resembling a pineapple. Milo nodded toward a small wooden table in the corner; its top painted artfully to masquerade as blue marble by a tenderly-remembered girlfriend of some years' removal.

"I meant that as an ambiguous someday in an undefined future, by which I mean time without end. For cryin' out loud, I quit less than a week ago. There's still beer in the keg from the party. The move started yesterday. I'm living out of boxes."

"But this is murder, Milo. Murder in a town where your standard garden-variety homicide is still the top story. And the guy who got murdered is a somebody. And doubly great the cops were called too late for the paper. You know the screaming headline tomorrow will be a 72 pointer."

"I can't bail on the guys. The Murphy bed is a beast."

Having shared an uncommonly enduring collaboration (by radio standards) of more or less collegial esprit de corps as a consequence of adjacent desks, Barry had long ago deduced Milo's Achilles heel. It was a vulnerability that could be pierced with skillful ego massage. He thrust.

"Come on, Milo. You are the best reporter in town. Hell, in all the Keys together. I add Miami to that. And when you put the word investigative in front of the reporter, you are the *goat*. Everybody knows it. I want nobody else on this story. We'll own it."

Milo understood he was being stroked but paused, considered the upside, and parried.

"Owning comes subsequent to purchasing."

Barry had wrangled accommodations from Milo for nearly two decades and could detect a diminishment of resistance. He jumped.

"How much?"

Milo wasn't reckless enough to fire the first shot in a duel over his market value. In the movies the gunslinger who draws first gets shot, and in *Hamilton* the first shot is a wasted shot.

"What's it worth to you?"

The phone went quiet for the time it took for Barry to mentally come up with a number and then subtract from it.

"I want you on this from start to finish. This is not some drunk-ass cruise ship dickhead getting knifed hitting on a shrimper's girlfriend at closing time. I see this playing out with you feeding up exclusive morsels day by day. Having said that, I also expect you to wrap it up in a nice bright bow with a big reveal a week from today. Eight days starting now. I can go seventy-five dollars a day plus reasonable expenses. And when I say reasonable, if I was texting that word to you it would be in all-caps."

Milo reasoned that murders seldom go unsolved in the Keys. The cops may already have a CCTV photo. How tough a job could this be? And he couldn't dispute that his PD had done him a solid, or at least a semi-solid, now and again. He enabled the speakerphone to include Mack and the Eskimo.

"Barry. We both know this gets packaged as a special report and you sell the sponsorship to Bishop Island Ford. Bruce Bishop can't find enough avails to buy as it is. Won't cost you a dime and it'll be a big shiny banner sales can carry into battle. You want to be first with the name of the killer and the motive. And that's going to take figuring out why the flipping flying fish somebody wants what got took. Let's say a flat two thousand for the week. I'll eat the expenses."

Barry winced at the thought of surrendering a single crumb of found money but Milo held the cards. And it crossed his mind he could double the revenue pitching Jolly Crossbones Bail Bonds as a co-sponsor. Perfect for a crime feature.

"Done. Get over there now. I want a piece for the noon."

"And a fifty buck voucher for Schooner Wharf."

"Milo," Barry whined. "Be a pal. We don't have a trade with them. They don't need it. Maybe in season." He sighed. "How about Ratlines? I can give you two forties."

Milo regarded Ratlines Rathskeller as overly dark and oddly alpine for Key West but free is free and the vouchers sealed the deal. Milo clicked off and searched for words that would not estrange that rarest genus of friends: volunteer movers.

Mack spoke first.

"Don't worry about it, Milo. Go. What are the odds? You eighty-six your job and two grand falls out of the sky."

"I still feel like a weasel, deserting you. I promise to spread the wealth. Let me collect the quick CSI quotes and start working it tomorrow. I'll be back by early afternoon to finish up here."

Mack turned to the Eskimo and said, "What about it? You heard." It was the Eskimo's nature to speak deliberately and with forethought, weighing his words. He took a last drag from his Dunhill, deftly flicked it out the door then brightened. "I heard there's still beer in the keg."

Chapter 2

Thirteen hours earlier

Nathan grumbled when the phone in his pocket blasted the sound of a ship's horn. He'd recorded it himself weeks ago as *Empress* pushed off from Pier B within sight of the bar where he was currently awaiting a refill of his Gentleman Jack. Nathan and his co-workers were mellowing at their Labor Day Weekend kickoff party at the Sunset Deck bar at the sprawling pierside resort. They were spread out across the rear of the bar, sequestered from the mob pressing to applaud wildly the sun's unvarying extinguishment. It was a short amble along the harbor promenade from their offices at the Old Custom House. The sun had vanished but happy hour had not and his attitude was properly adjusted to the next three days off the clock. He'd assigned the horn blast as the tone signaling a push notice from the museum security app.

   The app reported that a silent alarm had detected motion on the museum's deserted second floor. The tech people had updated app software and some vexing glitch had been activating sporadic alarm notices. After three false alarms police suggested employees check on the alarms and save them the manpower till the problem was resolved. Nathan was associate web content manager for Arts and Tourism. His boss was spending the holiday with family in Orlando and had given him the phone with the security controls. Nathan knew he could disable the alarm with a touch but protocol was protocol and the rule was no alarm went unchecked. Peeved, he displayed the screen alert to his companions, asked them to count him in for the next round, and with haste descended the stairs and double-quick-stepped the hundred yards to the museum. At least this time he wouldn't have to backtrack from home.

He'd waited an hour after the departure of the employees from the building. From his hiding place he heard the doors being locked and his concealment was made absolute when the museum lights were switched off. A small baseboard nightlight in the hallway dimly illuminated the gallery in which he had concealed himself hours earlier, reclining comfortably enough beneath an apron-wrapped display table. He had filled the time recalling verses of poetry he had committed to memory during long periods of enforced solitude as a result of unanimous verdicts. This recitation was The Highwayman. *Blood-red were his spurs in the golden moon; wine-red was his velvet coat, When they shot him down on the highway, Down like a dog on the highway, And he lay in his blood on the highway, with a bunch of*

lace at his throat. He liked the rhythm of it. He turned to
what he'd learned of Wreck of the Hesperus. He'd
nailed down thirteen of the quatrains. *Lashed to the
helm, all stiff and stark, With his face turned to the
skies; The lantern gleamed through the gleaming snow
On his fixed and glassy eye.* Nine more to master.

As he cautiously emerged he could see the LED
twenty feet above in the corner of the ceiling indicating
the motion detectors had been activated. He wasn't
concerned about them. This was the fifth time in eight
days he had remained undetected after hours and had
swiftly exited first floor doors to trigger the alarms, at
different times and in different locations. The police had
never arrived to rattle doors in sooner than five minutes.
The previous day cops had ignored the alarm and a
staffer showed up to investigate after twenty minutes.
This time he was concealed deeper within the building,
on the second floor. Which is where, with luck, it was.
A simple grab and dash, really. But he wanted to make
sure he had breathing room. He calculated that nine
minutes would be time enough.

He crept from concealment within the small gallery
and his eyes adjusted to the dull glow from the hallway.
He had slipped on black nitrile gloves before entering
the gallery. Latex gave him a rash. He activated the
flashlight on his phone. Steps away was a heavy green
rope of velour draped between two polished chrome
stanchions. An arm's length behind the rope, side by
side along the wall, were three wooden cabinets nearly
chest high. He moved a stanchion aside and opened the
cabinet door of the nearest. Within were four drawers.
He counted thirty objects in a single drawer and

assumed he would find a similar number in each. He
unzipped a canvas backpack and swiftly transferred the
objects three at a time. In the second cabinet there were
fewer objects and the transfer was accomplished in less
than half a minute. The third cabinet was locked. He'd
been prepared for that and lifted a lid on the top of the
cabinet and peered inside. A few seconds later he found
a key held by a clip mounted within. It took a minute to
empty the contents. He could have identified the single
object he wanted, but had precious few moments to
make his way through the gloom to the ground floor and
out. With no time to squander examining each, he took
them all.

    As he zipped the bag he heard it. A sound in a big old
empty building resonates. And this was not a small
sound. A door slammed somewhere below and he heard
purposeful footsteps on creaky floorboards followed by
a clatter of shoes ascending the grand staircase. The
stairs emerged onto the second floor just outside his
hiding place. He had no weapon. He had not anticipated
a need. He chose to run the chance of a simple breaking-
and-entering charge in the unlikely event of a police
encounter. This was no police encounter. He could duck
back under the table, but a flick of a light switch would
reveal the open cabinets. Exposure would place at risk
the entire enterprise. No. Swift and decisive action was
necessary. He unclipped the velvet rope from one of the
stanchions and hefted the post. The weight on the base
felt substantial. Probably cast iron. Thirty pounds at
least. He grasped it by the top of the post and held it like
a batter about to bunt; weighted base end-out. As the
footsteps grew louder and nearer, with a focused stride

he stepped into the hallway, took four accelerating giant steps toward the second floor landing and swung the heavy truncheon as the shadow of a man appeared at the top of the stairs. It was like swinging a barbell and the crushing weight would have done the job no matter where it hit. Where it hit was just beneath the throat and he could hear the collarbone shatter and uppermost ribs crack.

The dark figure lurched backwards as though struck by a train and the body slammed into and over the staircase baluster. The momentum of the weight's arc took it smashing down the stairs, its jouncing percussion causing the hollow steel stanchion to clang like a deathly chime, bong, bong, bong, filling the empty museum with its terrible clamor until it was stopped by a wall on the first floor in close proximity to the body it had broken.

Without a glance down the staircase he retrieved his bag. After a moment's deliberation and without panic, he changed his exit plan and made his way down the fire stairwell to avoid leaving bloody shoe prints. From the backpack he extracted a floppy fishing hat to shield his face from local surveillance cams. From somewhere up Front Street came the sound of a steel drum tapping out something familiar but indistinct. *Guava Jelly*? The breeze off the Gulf was warm on his face.

Chapter 3

The teal guayabera and cream linen trousers he was already wearing were tolerable as Key West work apparel. As were his gray canvas boat shoes. But Milo meant to steer clear of a fractious exchange with the peevish medical examiner; a glowering misanthrope quick to take offense. So he put on socks.

Milo paused by the Schwinn chained to the porch and considered pedaling to the crime scene. It was a holiday weekend. An unpredictable surge of out-of-towners could toss the parking situation into the lap of the gods. Still, early Saturday was customarily tranquil as the town slept off overnight shenanigans. The Healey would be quicker. It turned out the streets were deserted as he rolled up to the donut shop on Eaton. A half dozen would suit his purpose. North on Whitehead and a left on Front brought him to the museum driveway and he motored around to the back. He planted his media placard on the dash, and the cop keeping away the looky-lous glanced incuriously and turned back to his texting.

As he unfolded his long-limbed six feet three inches
from the waist-high ragtop, balancing his notepad atop
the donut box, a movement on his periphery drew his
attention to a solitary figure in the center of the plaza
beside the harbor. The man wore a stained and over-
large shirt and ragged shorts and his sneakers had no
laces. He was dancing to whatever melody was playing
in large and archaic headphones bridging his head.
Sometimes he would hop on one foot and then would
bend at the waist with arms out sideways and swoop
forward like a child playing airplane. For a moment
Milo considered giving him an unsolicited donation but
decided no; best not interrupt the dance. Like other
naturalized Conchs, Milo esteemed Key West as a
refuge where it was understood one and all are granted
the latitude to paddle his and her own canoe. A
sanctuary, where— like shooting irons had to be
checked with the sheriff in Old Tombstone—in Key
West intolerance is checked at mile marker 4.1. To be
sure, sometimes the price to be paid for being left alone
undisturbed is keeping a closer check on one's own
inclination to be a Judgy McJudge-pants. Because if
elsewhere people share memes that begin "Dance like
no one is watching…" the island version might start,
"Give a stranger a blow job in your front yard like no
one is watching."

The Old Custom House is an impressive pile of red
bricks built to nineteenth-century federal government
standards, which is why the roof is steeply pitched to
induce snow to tumble off and why a dozen fireplaces
were installed in a location where the average winter day
achieves an afternoon high of seventy-six. Over more

than a century it was the workplace of U.S. Customs
officials, federal district judges, postal workers and
Navy brass before assuming the responsibility of
allowing no random tourist strolling in from a cruise
ship to escape without knowledge of, one, what started
the Spanish-American War; two, the Great hurricane of
1935; and three, that once you could take a train here
and now you can't, because of number two.

As Milo stepped onto the porch at the museum
entrance, he met Herb Shrum departing. Herb wore his
usual suit of camel brown and cowhide bolo tie looped
through a clasp of agate the color of a school bus.
Resentful of the cards he was dealt as a short squat man
in a taller man's world, he refused to abase himself by
having to raise his head to make eye contact. He spoke
in the direction of Milo's shirt pocket.

"Oh. Bird." The medical examiner sniffed and
scowled, disappointment in his tone. "I heard you were
gone. And yet here you are. Ah, well. Hope deferred."
Milo opened his box. Shrum inspected the contents and
lifted a glazed. Wordlessly he turned and led Milo inside
and to the interior hallway. He paused where police tape
cordoned a perimeter surrounding the portion of the
hallway adjacent to the spattered staircase. The body bag
had been carried away and cleaners were busy.

Milo opened the recorder app on his home screen and
pressed a red dot. He raised his phone to Shrum's mouth
as he spoke without prompting.

"I think Mr. Parker met the heavy end of a steel
crowd-control rope post swung like a Louisville Slugger
as he reached the top step up there. It happened so fast
even the initial blood spatter from lower throat and chest

followed him down and backwards, over the handrail and to the stairs below, where more blood subsequently exsanguinated from multiple other wound sites as his impact was more or less headlong."

"So he died in the fall?"

"I would hazard a guess that if death was not instantaneous, the victim would have been more surprised than in any appreciable pain up till moment of death."

Examiner Shrum was satisfied that this response concluded the interview and took a bite from his donut, as Milo asked, "And when did it happen?"

Herb, annoyed, this time locked his eyes on Milo's and with intended discourtesy chewed slowly until at last swallowing before replying, imperiously, "That moment, judging from a preliminary exam and more importantly from the previous night's timeline, was between seven and nine. And any further speculation will come not from me but from the lead officer. I suggest you inconvenience the detective. "

Herb Shrum and his donut exited.

A uniform rounded the corner; a familiar face. "Hi, Bob. Who's the lead?"

"Jack Matthews." Bob turned and hollered, "Hey Jack! Got a minute? Milo Bird."

Detective Matthews appeared from the door of the gift shop. "Thought you quit. I have a hazy memory of being at a going away party."

"Just when I thought I was out, they pull me back in. Working this as a favor."

"Well, not much to know aside from the obvious. Nathan Parker comes back from a staff party at Sunset

Deck to check on an alarm. He assumes it was a false alarm. My keen deductive abilities have led me to the finding that his was a false assumption. Somebody from the party found him after he didn't return and didn't pick up."

"Any idea who did it and how come?"

"Haven't a clue. Actually, there is a clue but I haven't a clue about what it means. I am currently detecting, as I am paid to do. I'm heading to the examiner's lab now and you know it's a trek to Grassy Key." Milo lifted the lid on the donut box and Jack detected a Canadian bacon. "See the museum guy upstairs. Name's Everett. He can tell you about the stuff that was disturbed. Makes no sense yet, but it will eventually. Probably. Maybe."

Milo squeezed past the police tape to the elevator and pressed two. On the second floor more tape was draped across the ornamental railing over which Parker had plunged, preventing entry to the staircase descending to where the body had fallen. A KWPD photographer was at work. Museum media flack Nolan Everett was tapping notes into a tablet in a small gallery off the corridor. In jeans and Polo shirt he was dressed for the holiday weekend, not work.

Milo recalled meeting the man at some charity event but introduced himself as a matter of course. "Detective Matthews said you might be kind enough to tell me what happened here." He clicked on the recorder and Everett, a facile public speaker, nodded and leaned easily into the mic.

"Terrible thing. Nathan was a good guy. Good at his job. Did you know him?"

Milo said the name didn't ring a bell and expressed condolences. Everett beckoned him into the room.

"This gallery is usually a permanent exhibit of Depression-era Key West paintings commissioned by the WPA. Watercolors and such. Curators have temporarily removed them for restoration work. Treatment for mold. Repairing stretchers. Paintings on wood have special problems. Anyway, while the artwork is away, there is a temporary exhibit in this space. We call it *Edison in Key West*. That's where something is missing."

Milo's gut reaction was to get straight to that, but years of sharpening his interview skills had engrained in him a discipline cautioning him to go slow and let an interview subject tell a story in his own good time. He turned to survey the photos and documents displayed on the walls and a row of wooden cabinets. "Is—or was— any of this stuff to-kill-for valuable?"

Everett frowned and appeared genuinely bewildered. "None of it. I don't get it." He stepped to the wall nearest. "Let me walk you through this gallery. Maybe some background will be useful. Maybe you can see what I can't. What do you know about Thomas Edison?"

Milo thought. "I guess general stuff at best. The greatest inventor and Wizard of Menlo and all that. Mainly that he's famous for having a light bulb go off over his head."

"Okay. So it turns out Thomas Edison had multiple connections to Key West over his lifetime." Everett touched an acrylic display case containing an enlarged black and white image. "This photo is of Edison on the Navy docks here during World War One. He stayed here

four months in 1918 to help the Navy research ways to
protect American ships from German submarines. He
came up with dozens of prototypes and working devices.
All very top-secret. An underwater microphone that
could detect the sound of a torpedo approaching from a
distance of fifty football fields. A shell fired when a
periscope popped up that would blast a cloud of oily
gunk that would stick to the scope like spray paint
blinding the U-boat commander. That sort of stuff. But
it occurs to me that this is off-topic and not why you're
here. In this job I'm inclined to be overly talky. I can't
imagine any of this can relate to a murder. What do you
want to know?"

Milo was inclined to agree with Everett and was
doubtful that an "aha!" moment would appear this early
in the game. But this was the way it always began;
directionless. He smiled, "Experience teaches that if I
narrow the conversation to what I think I want to know,
I shut out most of what I *ought* to know. So if you have
the time I'll take the unabridged tour. The whole Edison
enchilada. Something brought a killer to this gallery and
at this point that something could be anything."

Everett shrugged, looked around, and moved on to a
document displayed on the adjacent wall. "Let's start
here. I expect you know that in the town's early days
Cuban cigar makers built factories here to avoid import
taxes. By the 1880s two thousand Cuban workers were
rolling more than sixty million cigars a year. By 1890
one third of everybody on the island was Cuban born.
Which is why we can still get a good café con leche all
over town. Cubans brought their own industry with them

and they took jobs away from no one and had money to spend so the locals had no beef with them. Until 1918."

Milo took a closer look at single framed handwritten page, accompanied by a printed transcription. Everett continued. "By all accounts Edison enjoyed his time in Key West. He was treated like the rock star he was and taken on sea trials and fishing excursions. But his wife hated it here. Her name was Mina. Rhymes with China. She despised Key West. She found it oppressively hot and dirty. She loathed the place. She especially loathed the Cubans. This is a letter from Mina to her son Theodore who was coming here to help his father experiment with weapons. She delivers a motherly warning about the dangers of Key West and says she was happy the Navy commandant and his wife took them into their home because their hotel was an oven and the streets were crowded with Cubans. At that time the flu pandemic of 1918 was blowing up and because it was called the Spanish Flu some here blamed the Cubans for its spread. Mina was one of those. She writes that she's heard the money is so contaminated by Cubans if one doesn't wash hands after handling it there's a risk of infection. She tried to be a good sport by joining the Navy wives social scene, but it was evident to her husband she was unhappy so he soon packed her off to their home in Fort Myers."

Everett turned back to Milo, his face conveying doubt that this ancient history was at all germane. Milo waggled a hand as a sign to carry on.

Nolan Everett moved on to a narrative account of Edison's time on the island and summarized, "Edison worked only on defensive technology. But his son Theo was also an inventor and worked on a secret weapon of his own design and tested it for months in isolation way out on Man Key. No photos exist, but from descriptions in family letters we had an artist sketch what it may have looked like. It was a wild contraption where a motor spun an explosive-filled wheel super fast on an axle. Then the axle was yanked out and the wheel zoomed across no man's land till it fell into the enemy trench and blew up. At least that was the idea. The Navy put him out there because his work was dangerous and involved frequently exploding TNT. It was never used."

Milo remembered scooting out to Man Key on a rented WaveRunner soon after arriving in Key West, unaware the marine sanctuary enfolding it posts an imaginary Keep-Out-Motorized-Watercraft barrier girdling all three hundred square miles of wildlife refuge. The Key—three tiny islands bobbing in the sea where the Straits meet the Gulf— is a haven to raucous birds and less vocal turtles; a small sliver of the USA south of the Southernmost monument and nine nautical miles distant from the nearest marauding raccoon. Milo was aware Teddy Roosevelt declared Man Key a refuge a decade before the Great War but could fathom why no one was inclined to begrudge the Edisons the ability to worry the birds with a little TNT. Whatever the war machines tested there, evidence of their presence is concealed beneath dense vegetation.

"Edison finished up his work here in April of 1918 and the war ended seven months later. The Navy never used any of his ideas. He was hacked-off about that for a long time. But he still submitted an invoice. And the Navy knew better, PR-wise, to try to stiff Thomas

Edison. By the way there was one big thing the Navy board headed by Edison did accomplish. It got all the industries in the country to standardize the sizes of screws and the pitch of their threads. Which is why you can find what you need in the screw aisle at Home Depot. But that war work wasn't his first Key West link."

Everett moved on to a photograph of a cameraman in suspenders cranking an old-timey camera affixed to a tripod.

"It could be said that Edison invented movie documentaries in Key West. He produced short subjects at his factory and the machines to play them were leased to saloons and pool halls. You put a nickel in and put your face over a viewer. They made a lot of money. Then the company came out with projectors. Less than two years after Edison's movies debuted in Vaudeville theaters the USS Maine blew up in Havana Harbor and Edison recognized an opportunity. He sent camera crews to cover the Spanish-American War. They captured the burial of the sailors killed on the Maine. Audiences were thrilled by the war scenes and packed into rooms where the films were screened. A number of the films were shot in Key West, which was where the Navy was staged for the war."

Everett pressed a touch-screen to start a video. "This is a looped Edison film clip of war correspondents leaping off a ship returning from Cuba and racing each other through Key West streets to the telegraph office to file stories." He turned back to Milo. "His cameramen filmed in Cuba but scenes of battle action were faked and shot in New Jersey using National Guard troops."

Everett was silent for a moment, then added, "Oh. Almost forgot. The year before the Maine blew up, Edison finished up installing the first electric lights here in a new Key West mansion. That's the one that tourists know as the Southernmost House."

At this point Everett had come to the end of the exhibits displayed on the gallery walls. Milo had been thoroughly engrossed in the account of local history unknown to him, but steered the matter back to the unfortunate Nathan Parker. "So what did you have on display here that may have gotten Parker killed? In your opinion."

Evert shrugged, bewildered. "That's the thing. Nothing. The things that got stolen were in here." He moved to the cabinet closest to him. "When we were planning the exhibit it was decided the photos and documents would be less static and pedantic a display if we added some Edison artifacts. We asked around among museum benefactors to see if any had antique Edison phonographs, but none did. So we contacted the Edison Winter Estate in Fort Myers and they were kind enough to loan us these three vintage players and cylinder recordings. We don't actually play them. We play a soundtrack of old cylinders that have been digitized. But it was the recordings that were cleaned out. From all three cabinets. Every one of them."

Chapter 4

Monday, July 29, 1929

Thomas Edison stepped from the freight elevator onto the top floor of West Orange Building Five and shuffled, unaided, into the expansive factory space that was the music room. It had been a busy time. The week before he had traveled to Chautauqua Lake in New York for a combined celebration of the 50th anniversary of his incandescent achievement and the 100th birthday of his late father-in-law, a founder of the Chautauqua social movement. Tomorrow began the Edison Scholarship competition. The inventor was 82 and unwell. He'd been fighting pneumonia all summer. His Bright's disease and diabetes caused him agonizing back pain. His face was puffy, legs swollen. Most people used catchall non-technical names for the conditions which afflicted him; among them cholera morbus and the collywobbles. Frequent bleeding turned his urine a smoky salmon. At irregular intervals he winced at a reignited inflammation from a gastric ulcer. Stomach pain robbed him of appetite. His diet was restricted to milk and

*orange juice. A year from now, his withering kidneys
would inflict uremia, poisoning his blood. In thirty
months, he would be dead.*

*Mort Hall, Phonograph Division chief of sales and
marketing, deferentially motioned Edison to take a seat
in a simple oaken spindleback chair at a worn wooden
table upon which was arrayed a variety of microphones.
Recordist Jerry Drumm had been reverse-engineering
some newly acquired RCA ribbons in current
development, but for this application he chose a proven
technology Western Electric double-button carbon; a
model 387. His boss was partial to the duralumin
diaphragm for voice reproduction. Edison had been late
to the party in the use of electrical impulses to drive the
recording stylus, relying with rock-ribbed obstinacy on
the mechanical force of air pressure in a diaphragm
which had been (literally) cutting-edge technology since
the day he shouted some Mother Goose into the horn of
a foil-wrapped cylinder machine more than a half-
century earlier.*

*Jerry ordinarily would tee-up a blank disc for a
master recording, even when the recording would later
be dubbed onto Blue Amberol cylinders. But this
recording session was extraordinary. He had rigged the
electronics to power a cylinder mastering cutter to
preserve the old man's spoken words the way it was
when recording was new: hill and dale across the tube.
It was integral to the symbolism of the project they do it
old school. Onto the recording mandrel he slipped the
first of the mastering cylinders he had arranged on the
table. Three in all, the number of times Edison would*

repeat the lines on the page. Of the three, the best would be used to create duplicates in multiple formats.

The old man, his famously snowy hair now thin and wispy, turned to his sales boss, who handed him a single sheet bearing lines of copy. Edison murmured the words aloud as the engineer made his adjustments, then the enfeebled national treasure leaned into the 387, and, with his nod, the recordist commenced the rotation of the cylinder. Leaning his face closed to Edison's head, his mouth nearly touching the deaf inventor's ear, Hall shouted, "This, sir, will be the cause of much excitement!" Edison turned his pale head, and arching an eyebrow resembling nothing so much as a bushy dark caterpillar, he winked, then faced forward and began to read. As the grooves were cut, the recordist brushed away the swarf; the hard celluloid residue removed by the cutting edge. These were Edison's words made visible, and they fell like rain.

Chapter 5

Gorse was surprised Cameron wasn't crazy mad over the unplanned killing. He seemed more interested in the reporter angle. Time and again he'd caught holy hell for more meaningless screwups. Gorse had been resolute in his assurance he'd left no trace. That the theft had not produced the cylinder was disappointing but of no real consequence. They had been there before. His boss directed that he check the local paper and monitor broadcasts to discover what was being made public.

Saturday afternoon Cameron nurtured the seed of an idea as his Man Friday reported tuning to a news and talk station listed on his rental's preset. There were a series of reports from the museum by a reporter including sound bites of official talking heads. Nobody spoke to motive. Nobody had a surmise about the significance of the stolen recordings. But Gorse related that the announcer at the station followed every report by repeating the reporter's name and making some ballyhoo over his reputation as an investigator. It was suggested this guy had exposed criminal conspiracies before and the on-air anchor warned that listeners tuning elsewhere would surely regret missing their man finding out about stuff in this case.

"This could play in our favor, Morris." Cameron was the only one who called Gorse by his first name. "We've been taking stabs in the dark. One long-odds shot after another. We know what we are looking for and nobody else does. Which is good. But we don't know how to find it. Which is bad. Maybe this Bird would have an idea. If we gave him an idea. A trained investigator working for us would be useful. If he doesn't know he's working for us."

Gorse thought about that. "If he finds it, what's to stop him from keeping it?"

"We'd need to keep him close. On a short leash. I have an idea about that. Your meeting with the collector in New Orleans? Put that aside. Stay where you are. Let me make inquiries about this Bird and call you back with a game plan. Right now he's clueless. Let's fix that."

The door was unlocked but the boys were gone when Milo returned home. A note informed they'd removed to Green Parrot and they'd save a seat at the bar. There remained boxes to unpack but the furnishing feng shui had been more or less accomplished. They'd even hooked up the electronics. Milo powered up the computer. He'd phoned in his audio pieces and he thought it pointless to squander time hypothesizing randomly without more information. But his inquiring nature overcame his resolve and he took a moment to

ask the great fountainhead of all knowledge what it had
to say about Thomas Alva Edison. It turned out to be
quite a lot. The search words Thomas and Edison
returned seventy-eight million results. Foremost was
Wikipedia, which cited the buzzwords Milo associated
with Thomas Edison. Wizard. Check. West Orange labs.
Check. Menlo lab at Henry Ford Museum. Edison
Florida home. Phonograph, incandescent bulb, movies,
batteries and on and on. Milo opened his word processor
and put on his thinking cap. Wading through the shitload
of Edisonia was a wasted effort. He switched gears and
shifted his center of attention to Nathan Parker. Herb
Shrum and Jack Matthews were restrained by procedure
to begin with forensics. That's where Milo's road
through the investigative yellow wood diverged. His
fact-finding toolbox included a well-exercised
imagination. He was permitted license to consider facts
not in evidence; straight-up guesswork. So he made up a
story. Parker was murdered because he had it coming.
The killer waited in the dark for Nathan Parker to arrive.
He knew he would respond to the intruder alarm,
because that's what he would have done if Parker had
not stolen the job he knew was rightly his. He had
worked for the council for years, and was stunned when
management picked an outside hire. It was a punch in
the gut betrayal. He hated Parker.

So the motive was personal. Maybe not that motive,
but still. Parker stole his girl. Parker killed his brother.
Parker bullied him in school. Parker spurned his
romantic overture. And the killer would deceive
investigators by giving the appearance of a burglary
gone bad. By stealing the first thing at hand. Milo's

inner editor took out a blue pencil and scratched theory one. It was constructed of sand and easily knocked down. After killing Parker on the landing, why waste time poking around in a side room looking for valuables. There are paintings on the walls. Other stuff. No way he would randomly open a cabinet door and gather up dozens of objects. He could have grabbed one object and accomplish a burglary. Something more desirable than obsolete cylinders. Milo visualized the collection of old records. He would have needed a bag to hold them. Couldn't carry them all without a container. So gathering the records was pre-planned. Had to be.

Milo typed the words "valuable Edison cylinder" into the browser. A collector blog informed that most are worth less than five dollars but that rare and desirable recordings such as historical figures speaking could bring five hundred. Not murder-worthy. Milo was confident a foundation would be laid. Lateral reasoning. What does this become when one adds this other thing? In the absence of anything solid, intuition suggested the places Edison worked and lived are where to begin. Somewhere there might lurk a reason one might have for killing over an old plastic record.

He transferred notes and the audio on his phone to a folder on the laptop and shut down. A beer sounded good.

The Lyft pulled away as Milo stepped into the Parrot's open door. Steve Earl was on the jukebox. Ceiling fans labored to move the heavy air. The heat of summer's end in Key West is oppressive only at intervals. The same dependable easterly breeze that filled the sails of European voyagers still triumphs over blazing sun to cool the skin most days. It was the reason the harbors reside along the island's more sheltered northwest. The usual suspects wrapped around a corner of the bar. Cal and Don Diego had joined Mack and the Eskimo. A scheduled endoscopy had given Ben an excused absence. Milo slipped onto the stool next to Cal. He waved to Vicki standing at the pulls. She waved back and reached for a pint glass.

Cal swiveled to bump a fist and say, "Breaking news has it you're buying."

"An extremely limited time offer. But yeah."

A discussion was in progress. The Eskimo had recounted cleaning a hull beneath a large pleasure boat the day before and that he'd seen a couple of nice sponges; a bell and a barrel. He observed he was seeing fewer of them. Then Mack asked had anyone seen the old sponge-hooker movie *Beneath the Twelve Mile Reef*. The members of the colloquium present took up the issue.

Don Diego: "Tarpon Springs Greeks against Key West Conchs. My dad watched them shoot a scene somewhere on the docks here. He took a picture with Gilbert Roland."

Mack: "Okay. Never in twenty years as an Army dive instructor here did I ever have to pull my knife on a giant octopus. That flick left moviegoers in Nebraska with the impression it was scary dangerous to get sponges on the Twelve Mile Reef because of the giant octopus."

Don Diego: "Maybe so, but how do you make raking sponges interesting without a giant octopus?"

The Eskimo: "I think Robert Wagner was pretty good the way he fought that octopus."

Mack: "But how do you cast Robert Wagner as a Greek?"

"Well, Gilbert Roland played his dad," said Don Diego. "And he was Mexican."

This was followed by a general murmur signifying a point made and a brief discussion of movies with good octopus knife fights. Mack was ruled out of order for including *20,000 Leagues Under the Sea* because that was a squid.

The discussion drifted companiably before dropping anchor at the topic of the museum murder. Milo had often employed his crew as a sounding board for his story research. Their disparate backgrounds provided multiple viewpoints that not infrequently resulted in avoiding tiresome legwork. None of the others listened to radio and Milo described his morning and the little he knew.

Cal processed the slender data.

"Ex nihilo nihil fit." He said.

They all sipped their drinks, waiting for it.

"The poet Lucretius wrote nothing can be created out of nothing. Each effect has a cause. We have arrived at the theater late and have missed the beginning of the play. We have come in during the second act and must reason out what came before *a posteriori;* from what comes later. There are two truths we can assume. Virgil wrote that a hunger may lead to crime. Whoever is acquiring these cylinders is feeding some hunger. And Juvenal wrote that one never becomes wicked suddenly; *nemo repente fuit turpissimus.*"

Milo smiled. "So you're saying I should be looking for a Juvenal delinquent."

Cal bumped a fist with Milo and said, "Quite right. The thief is no stranger to malign fuckery. I assume it is a man. From its savagery. He will take extraordinary risks to acquire these objects which are of no obvious value. He knows something we don't. But you can be sure he's doing what he's doing for a very good reason."

Monty "Cal" Calloway was a retired bridgetender who had migrated to Key West from Chicago. For thirty years he had raised and lowered the 95th Street Bridge on the city's south side. Cal was a thickset fuzzy bear with a barrel chest and arms a mass of white curly hair. Irish by ancestry, the tropical sun painted his face and forearms a florid shade of not-quite-ripe strawberry. He had a dermatologist on speed dial.

Time passes slowly for a bridgeman. Hours can pass without a boat requiring passage. So Cal built a floor-to-ceiling bookcase on the floor below the control tower and its contents grew to thousands of books borrowed and bought over three decades. He taught himself languages. He also painted. His bar mates regarded him as the go-to egghead when Jeopardy was on.

The crew of six evolved organically as bar posses do. Its genesis is a shared affinity among strangers for a bar and a preferred day-part. Protocol dictated that newcomers sit a respectful distance from established stool-warmers over a probationary period during which one discerns which drinkers will abide human contact. The trial period concludes when one's entrance draws nods of recognition from regulars. In time, one is cautiously auditioned for associate membership by inclusion in conversation, which is an invitation to move a stool closer. Band brotherhood is achieved when regulars solicit an authentic personal opinion and names are formally exchanged.

The brotherhood ping-ponged at unfixed intervals between a couple of preferred saloons. This one was once a hangout for submariners living at the Navy base close by. When the Navy downsized the installation locals and bikers claimed it as it was re-branded Green Parrot. Playboy wrote of it, "The management works tirelessly to avoid progress." Veteran barflies took pride in loyalty to the dive that Hemingway, when in residence a few blocks away, walked past every day on his way to Sloppy Joe's.

The talk shifted to the compulsory topic of the itinerary of Tropical Storm Maxine. In the face of cyclones Key West is battled-tested and displays a devil-may-care moxie verging on the foolhardy. The island has ducked many direct hits but multiple ferocious storms have made landfall within spitting distance. So when a blip appeared on the map off Cape Verde five days ago and began moving in a more or less direct path toward the Green Parrot, attention was paid. Happily, at six days out Maxine gave no appearance of going full-on Hulk and was forecast to pass a good ways north of Key West as, at most, a category two. For many Conchs, a two is not even shutter-worthy.

The jukebox queued up a succession of John Lee Hooker, Velvet Underground and some vigorous Taj Mahal harmonica as the soundtrack to bar talk in advance of Milo's exit. He left cash on the bar to underwrite continuing intemperance and let it be known

that, despite the holiday weekend, for him tomorrow
was a work day.

Chapter 6

It was twilight and street lights cast shadows through a
canopy of gumbo limbo and dogwood when Milo
climbed the porch stairs to his home. Stepping inside he
flipped the switch inside the door. Darkness remained.
Annoyed, he left the door open to cast a pale streak of
light across the floor. He entered the room and paused
for his vision to adjust before confronting the
disobedient lamp.

Milo felt a meaty arm snake around his neck and haul
him backward into an unseen and solid torso. The arm
flexed beneath his jaw and the back of a strong open
hand completed the circle around his throat pressing
hard below his ear. A second hand gripped the back of
his head and pushed it forward into the crook of the
tightening arm. The hidden man bore down with his
heavy head pressed into the back of Milo's skull to
leverage the pressure against the carotids. The invader's
humid breath was dank upon his neck. Milo jabbed an
elbow backward to where he guessed he would find the
attacker's gut, but in seconds strength abandoned his

limbs and his vision became indistinct. As Milo's consciousness dimmed, his assaulter pivoted and hurled his captive to the side. The thrust propelled Milo over the back of a couch where he landed as dead weight on the cushion and rolled off onto the floor. Blood returned to his brain and his eyes observed a diffuse and dreamy shadow solidify into the foot of a leg on his coffee table.

The bushwhacker had fled. His head rested on a shoulder. "Lucky," he thought. His own flopping arm saved his skull from playing percussion on the hardwood. Woozy and off balance, he pulled himself onto the couch and breathed. The fog cleared. Milo pulled his phone from his pocket, scrolled through contacts and touched a name. Detective Jack Matthews.

With Jack on the way, Milo tightened the bulb that had been unscrewed in the lamp, and walked through the apartment looking for anything out of place. There was no clear evidence of mischief. A desk drawer was not firmly closed. Ditto his bedroom chest of drawers. He would have to examine the contents of the remaining packing cartons but there was no observable indication of ransacking.

His laptop was closed and powered down, as he had left it, but it was not password protected. The intruder could have poked around. He turned it on and navigated to the event log. The event viewer recorded unspecified activity around twenty minutes earlier. Corroboration of a trespass. Milo surveyed the front room again. He had forgotten the front door was still partially ajar, and as he moved to close it he noticed, on the floor behind it, a small slip of folded paper. Lined paper ripped from a small note pad. Milo unfolded and smoothed its creases.

On it were scrawled in artless cursive the words:
*Contest-1929-Edison-Ford-Firestone-Hathaway-Find
cylinder.*

They talked outside to keep clear of the forensic
technician sniffing out trace evidence. "I got clobbered."
Milo leaned forward in a slat-backed walnut rocker on
his front porch as Jack Matthews took notes, his two-
hundred pounds supported by the rear two feet of a chair
of unknown hardwood propped to lean back against the
front wall. It was cane-seated and acquired for six
dollars at a yard sale. Milo had painted it bright orange
and blue. Matthews was considered by some to be
handsome. Not movie star handsome, but broad-
shouldered and solid with a disarming grin that could
reel in a vacationing professor of English Lit over the
course of a happy hour. He preferred relationships of the
Airbnb three-night-stay variety.
    "You should get checked out," said Jack.
    "I'm okay. Maybe a little black and blue tomorrow,
but I'm okay." He'd already described the attacker as
best he could without having seen his face. A strong
man with a big upper body and muscled arms. Like a
guy who pumps iron. The position of the intruder's head
pressing into him from behind suggested he was shorter
than Milo, by as many as several inches. But heavier.
And there was an odor. A lightly fragrant scent. He
couldn't place it but he knew it. "Like an aftershave
you'd get at Christmas from an aunt. A little whiff of
something acrid like turpentine. But mostly the smell of
eucalyptus."

"So we're looking for a guy built like a gorilla who smells like koala piss."

"If you have that guy in a lineup I could sniff him out blindfolded."

Milo kept the discovery of the folded paper to himself. He wasn't ready to surrender it to the gendarmes before considering its implications. He needed time to noodle it. But he'd give Matthews something else to chew on. "The guy was in my computer. I don't know what he did or what he was looking for. I wouldn't know how to do it but it would be useful to know what he did while he was rooting around."

"Right. So if you can spare the laptop I'll take it with me and our IT guy will get into it. Don't expect he'll be in on the holiday but I'll get it back soon as he's done."

"Great. I can work with my tablet till then."

Milo felt like he'd just gotten off the table after ninety minutes with the world's worst massage therapist. The withholding of blood to his brain left him with a piercing headache and a dull pain behind his eyes. His neck hurt and the impact with the floor had bruised a hip. After Matthews departed Milo reckoned morning was soon enough to put his aching head back to work. He pulled down the Murphy bed for the first time in his new home and collapsed into his pillow and into a deep and dreamless sleep.

Sunday morning arrived amidst gleaming rain-washed sunshine. A storm had passed on toward the Marquesas leaving behind freshness in the air evocative of linen straight from the drier and the sounds of lingering dribbles from tree limbs splashing upon metal rooftops. Save for a stiff neck Milo felt reasonably restored after coffee and a stale donut.

He recorded and filed a brief report describing his home invasion and suggesting a connection to the death at the museum. Soon after he received a text from Barry. Absent was any expression of concern about his injuries. Barry was exultant about the new development. The mugging made the story more than ever about the radio station. He was beside himself with joy.

Milo spent the early morning organizing his lines of inquiry. He created a list of questions suggested by the weekend's episodes. And beside them, he began construction of a list of sources that could provide the A's to his Q's. He created a logbook file in his phone notepad, but his custom was to make a visual representation of accumulating facts employing index cards pinned to a corkboard.

Legwork to a reporter had changed fundamentally since Milo trekked to police precincts to grovel before desk sergeants and supplicate for a peek at incident reports and arrest logs. He recalled years of scuffing shoe leather knocking on doors of addresses in the notes scrawled in longhand by cops at the scene. The police scanner chatter which suffused every newsroom with an atmosphere of authentic immediacy had been silenced by departments that encrypted cop-to-dispatch radio. Now police reports arrived in inboxes, gussied-up and typos fixed by PIOs, and sometimes entire investigations were completed start to finish in cyberspace. Milo's questions were few. Why did someone kill over a couple of dozen ancient records? Who is that killer? What is the

Edison record that was the killer's target? What audio does it contain? What is the contest of 1929?

Edison, Ford, Firestone, Hathaway. He typed those names into a search engine. There appeared many hits connecting the first three names but below the result the word Hathaway was struck through and reported "missing."He thought back to a few years ago when correlating facts was a bit more time consuming than asking an algorithm to fish the sea of knowledge and haul out word associations in an instant. Another reason to quit before being replaced by a robot. Investigative reporting used to mean expense accounts, traveling, libraries, newspaper microfiche. Now anybody with opposable thumbs and a clue can do it.

He hunted up an aggregation of contacts at a number of places associated with Edison that still offer gift shops and media relations offices and with mild surprise found them in abundance. It struck Milo that, in addition to creating landmark inventions of science and industry, Tom also created an entire cultish tourism industry. He shot off an email to the Edison birthplace in Ohio, where young Tom watched Lake Erie cargo schooners glide by on the Milan Canal. Another to the Thomas Edison Center and monument at Menlo Park; now Edison State Park in Edison Township. Likewise The Henry Ford Museum in Michigan, where Edison acolyte Henry relocated buildings and lab equipment from both Menlo and Edison's Florida lair. He was especially interested in connecting with Thomas Edison National Historical Park in West Orange, New Jersey, where an immense walk-in refrigerator with vault-like intruder and fire protection stores eleven thousand cylinder records, twenty-eight thousand disc records, thirty-five hundred notebooks in Edison's hand and other stuff like the warehouse in *Raiders of the Lost Ark*.

He also imagined it worth a call to somebody at Rutgers, where archivists were still sorting through five million Edison personal and business documents. And maybe some librarian honcho at The University of California in Santa Barbara, curating an online collection of more than two terabytes of digitized Edison cylinders.

He sent introductory notes explaining his purpose and requesting a chat. Milo was aware that it was unlikely any of the media PR flacks would return his message over a long holiday weekend. But there was a place he could go for answers without delay. He'd confirmed the Edison-Ford Winter Estates remain a popular Labor Day attraction and he'd resolved to take off for Fort Myers in the afternoon. There was method in starting at the Fort Myers home. It was the museum that had loaned the stolen cylinders to Key West. And a paragraph appearing in the Fort Myers Wikipedia page described how, when the local vaudeville theater was built, Edison and his bosom pals Henry Ford and Harvey Firestone would go there together to see movies. Edison, Ford, Firestone. *Three out of four*.

Chapter 7

Griffin "Griff" Cameron was a child of post-Castro
South Florida. He arrived as Gaspar Zaldivar and was
two years-old and seasick in his mother's arms when she
struggled off a rusty lobster boat from Mariel and onto
Key West and into a bus that carried them both to the
Orange Bowl. They spent days camped with numberless
refugees beside the Miami River. Their ceiling, the
Interstate 95 elevated span soaring hundreds of feet
overhead, shielding them from soaking, hurricane-
season rains. His mother would retell relentlessly the
story of the church van that appeared and of the people
in the van who gave Griff brand new blue jeans and
tennis shoes. They were U.S. Keds, and his mother told
him he was now a U.S. kid.

When the Zaldivars were at last taken in by cousins
in West Miami, the young Marielito from Matanzas
zealously copied what he took to be U.S. kid behavior
from a series of adolescent role models. Role models
who were periodically removed from the streets to
receive tutoring in advanced migrant survival skills by
instructors inhabiting the juvenile justice system. He

observed that success on the outside more frequently eluded internees who resisted assimilation. Despite his habitual commissions of infractions that now and again took him out of circulation, he resolutely made every effort to Americanize. In the forty years since that ninety-mile boat ride, Gaspar had almost no trace of an accent and bought his clothes at Nordstrom, leaving the guayaberas to players of bongos and dominoes.

Serving a two year term for stealing a boat, Griff had taken a prison workforce re-entry course in computer programming and discovered to his surprise that he had a natural aptitude for coding and software problem solving. From fellow techie yardbirds he became convinced that computer crime would be his ticket to prosperity; to achieving his aspirational mantra to "Out angle the Anglo." A long-termer cellmate tutored him in the basic elements of his first scam.

He misappropriated the identity of a Miami-Dade retiree who moved to Costa Rica to join the ex-pat community. Becoming Griffin Cameron resolved the nuisance of criminal background checks.

Next, he bought a fifty-dollar pop-up canopy tent with sidewalls and a ten dollar table. He printed an appealing vacation contest poster for a trip for two to a Bahamas resort he poached from a travel site and taped it to a cardboard easel. He purchased generic entry registration pads and a prize wheel online, wrapped a box in white paper and cut a hole for insertion of entry forms.

Community calendars revealed times and locations of large street fairs with hundreds of tents. He'd scout an empty space beside a legitimate exhibitor and set up early. With the trap set, he left a printed notice in large letters on the table reading, "Back in an hour." He scattered a half-dozen pens across the table and departed. If event officials noticed an unauthorized participant there was no one to confront. Returning after hours, he would find the box stuffed with hundreds of names, phone numbers and email addresses.

To those he would text and email overdue library notices with links to ransomware that would disable phones and computers until payment was received.

After enjoying steady income from his library scam, it occurred to Griff that libraries likely had minimal budgets for online security and found it a piece of cake to hack into their library card member databases. Here, he harvested thousands more names and contact information from the comfort and cover of his apartment at zero expense. A great number of regular users of libraries were seniors unschooled in online hazards. Scammers called it shooting phish in a barrel.

Dazzled by the movie Scarface and its story of another Cuban refugee outlaw's rise to power and wealth in Miami, Griff moved from Little Havana to a townhouse in historic old Miami. If Freedom Town tent city success story Tony Montana found Coconut Grove good enough for him, it was good enough for Griff. The mansion would come later.

Ambitious, Griff printed business cards and stationery and created a web site purporting to be a computer services consulting company. Businesses across Florida were adapting to serve a bi-lingual consumer base. *Unfolding Web Technologies* promised a bogus solution to companies wishing to provide a

Spanish translation of their web pages to Latino visitors. He pitched superior translating accuracy at cut-rate cost. It was a breeze to double-talk top-tier corporate execs. Most had the Spanish language aptitude of a five year-old. When a company let him in the door for a demonstration, he would idle away a few days pretending to implement complex coding. In truth he installed in minutes a freeware bare-bones translation application into the web code. This provided him hours of access to company databases where he copied anything of value. If left alone he also searched file cabinets for secrets and data that might be of value on the dark web. If he spied physical objects of value, he called Gorse, who would acquire the objects after a suitable passage of time.

Griff met Gorse in prison where he was serving five years for involuntary manslaughter, which in point of fact had been sure-as-hell voluntary, but had produced inconclusive evidence. Cameron likewise was remorseless, initiating extreme measures when reckoned advantageous.

When he'd completed his charade of upgrading a web server and had completed his reconnaissance, Griff demonstrated the translation conversion of the client site with mediocre results, which he abjectly attributed to a server's incompatibility with his system. With apologies, he removed his program and departed after recommending a legitimate company they might consult.

Having failed to win a contract and withdrawing unpaid, his looting of company secrets went undetected by clients who had moved on. It was in this way Griff discovered the Edison contest.

He'd wangled entrée to the Edison-Ford Winter Estates offices with the offer of a free-no-strings demonstration of his translation software. He was given three weeks to install and test and found it on the second day.

The documents were among those tucked into a manila envelope in an old wooden file cabinet in a room in the Edison complex that had been converted to storage. The cabinet had evidently been banished here when a glut of folders had ended its usefulness. The envelope contained a collection of white on black photographic reproductions of written records. An explanatory note described the contents as photostats taken of Edison printed matter donated to the Henry Ford Museum. There, originals had been placed into desk drawers and bookcases on display in the Edison buildings for added authenticity. In the pre-Xerox epoch, museum archivists created negative images of the loaned materials and returned them to the Fort Myers lab as a record of what had been donated. He was drawn to two documents. One, a handwritten summary of a departmental meeting. The other extended across several pages, displaying columns of bank accounts. Descriptors suggested they were defunct accounts initially created to fund Edison marketing projects at the West Orange HQ. Most were marked closed as projects were completed. Some were marked closed because the projects were abandoned. But one account had not been marked closed. Its label described it as funds in the form of one hundred shares of stock from each of four companies, set aside as a prize purse for a project titled "Edison Records Contest, 1929." A handwritten notation directed to "see recording sec. minutes descript." And its space in the Account Total column was filled with a question mark instead of a dollar amount. He copied the account number and the holder, J.P. Morgan & Co.

He phoned a fellow alumnus of the prison computer class, a one-time cellmate who had been hired as a Wall Street corporate cyber-security expert precisely because he had a criminal record for cyber-mischief. It took a single day of networking for him to track down the account, now administered by Morgan Stanley, and to identify it as still active. The phone in Griff's hand trembled as he heard the current account balance.

Chapter 8

Milo's fingers maneuvered clumsily across the onscreen keyboard. Several corrections later he touched send on his final media query and shut down his iPad. He slipped it into his backpack and was folding a change of clothes when he heard footfalls on the porch and a knock on the door. He hoped it was Mack with the laptop but knew it was wishful thinking. He called out from the bedroom, "It's not locked."

She was framed in light, backlit in the tropical sun, her outline giving the appearance of generating the brightness that surrounded her. She was a happy surprise, like a June bloom on a Christmas cactus; pretty as a floater on a daiquiri. She stood in the door, her slender arms crossed at her waist, one hand clasping its kindred wrist. She was dressed in what in Key West passes for business formal. A waist-length single-button sunflower-yellow blazer over a white scoop neck top, white cotton pants encasing slender legs to just above her ankles. She wore flats, like a ballet dancer. Her hair was dark blonde with shades of wheat. It was cut short

and descended asymmetrically to frame the corners of
her smile with wisps of curls. Had she been smiling. Her
face and stance were purposeful. She appeared to mean
business, in an unaffectedly adorable way.

"Milo Bird? The guy who does Early Bird News?"

Milo said, "I'm Milo, but that bird has flown. I quit
the station. I'm just settling into my new roost."

"Hi. My name is Danny Carreras. I write for Diario
Las Americas. I spoke with Barry Richards at the station
and he said I would find you here."

Mildly annoyed Barry hadn't given him a heads-up,
Milo wasn't surprised by the appearance of a reporter
unannounced. It was his custom, too, to brace an
interview subject cold. Calling ahead provided
opportunity for dodging a meet-up or to invite a straight-
up "Fuck off." Even now, humans were inclined to be
polite face to face.

Milo stepped to the door and politely motioned for
her to enter. Closing the door he said, politely, "You
almost missed me. I was just about to take off. "

"I'm sorry to be a bother. I just drove down from
Miami and imagined you might be kind enough to give
me some information. I saw a reference in the Herald to
your report on the murder here and couldn't help but
wonder if it could be connected to some incidents I've
been following in Miami-Dade."

Her lips were parted slightly even in repose, as
though about to blow gently on a dandelion. Milo tossed
empty packing boxes off the couch to make room and
directed her to sit. "Try to ignore the clutter," he said,
"I'm moving in." He turned a chair to face her as she
continued.

"There have been some burglaries in Miami. Little Havana mostly and not much out of the ordinary. Just routine police blotter stuff but the beat reporter noticed an odd link between two of them; the mention of old Latin music cylinder records among the items stolen. My editor assigned me to do a light piece on why on earth people in the Cuban community still keep such old records and what was on them. When the Key West murder broke he sent me down to find what I can on what went missing here. I was on the way to the Custom House but thought it would be a good idea to first pick the brain of the guy who broke the story."

There was a rise and fall of melody in the way she spoke. The pitch of her voice ascended to complete her statements as if they were questions.

"I can't imagine our audiences overlap," said Milo, "I can share what little I know, but I expect to know more soon. I'm just freelancing this one last story for Barry. Like you, I'm going on a field trip to hunt up some enlightenment." He thoughtfully dissected her story, dubious about Hispanic market demand for wax cylinders more than a hundred years ago.

As though reading his mind, Danny said, "Do you know if any of the cylinders taken here were Spanish language? I was surprised to find out that Edison founded the Mexican National Phonograph Company in Mexico City in 1906 and sold capital stock to set up the Compania Edison Hispano Americana in 1907. It had a branch office in Buenos Aires that sold records and record players and movies and projectors across South America. Edison did a pretty good business in records with Spanish singers and not only in Latin America.

Immigrants to the U.S. played them till they were worn
down as memories of home."

He shook his head. "I have no answer to that," said
Milo, "but I will tomorrow. I'm heading up to the
Edison home in Fort Myers this afternoon. The cylinders
that were lent to the Custom House came from there and
a media staffer promised to put together an inventory of
the titles for me. We meet up in the morning. I'll share
the list when I have it. I'll poke around and hope to find
some flicker of a hunch about why these things are
suddenly a hot commodity."

Danny brooded for a moment without speaking,
looking at the floor as she thought it over. She raised her
head and met Milo's eyes with her own. Brown eyes
flashed earnestly and her brows narrowed. She said,
with a pouty smile of contrition, "Umm…Look. I really
don't mean to be a bother, but can I come with you?
From what you say there is more of a story to find in
Fort Myers than here. Cross my heart I won't get in
your way and if you have questions to ask you don't
want me to hear I'll make myself scarce."

Milo was not given to rejecting requests from
beautiful women. He could not imagine a downside and
it would be nice to have company on a tiresome road
trip. He would keep the subject of a 1929 contest to
himself. She could ask her own questions.

It was agreed she would retrieve her overnight bag
from the bargain-basement B&B her editor had
approved and would follow Milo to the mainland, where
she would leave her car at the junction of Tamiami Trail
and join him for the run up to Fort Myers. He'd

considered and dismissed the notion of traveling by
boat.

"There's a big catamaran that runs back and forth
between Fort Myers and the marina a few blocks from
here. The upside is that it's faster than driving. The
downside is that it only runs to Key West once a day.
We could board before sunset and be in Fort Myers in
four hours. But the next boat back is at eight in the
morning. The Edison museum doesn't open till nine. So
we'd be stuck in Fort Myers two nights." Milo fleetingly
considered possibilities that might present themselves in
the course of a two-night hotel stay in the company of
Danny Carrerras. "But if we drive we'll arrive tonight
and you can be back in Miami in daylight."

When she reappeared on his porch she had changed
to sky blue jeans that ended mid-calf and a clingy
scooped tangerine tank. Velvet skin descended from her
throat to a stingy display of bosom.

The convoy departed.

Milo had left Florida City in his rearview mirror
followed by his escort, who, in fact, was driving a white
Ford Escort of indeterminate age. The way north was
wide open, as the Labor Day mob was bound for the
Keys. They were now on the turnpike tracing the official
hurricane evacuation route out of the chain of islands.
Monroe County commands the Keys be abandoned
when the forecast is for a Cat 3 and up. Maxine was
predicted to stay a 2 and wouldn't arrive for another five
days. He'd last taken this route during Irma when he
broadcast from the Keys' designated storm shelter, a
large, hangar-like exhibition hall at the Miami-Dade
Fairgrounds. The big reinforced barn of a structure was

the destination of huddled masses of refugees who couldn't or wouldn't spring for self-indulgent pampering at sundry hotels offering sumptuous snug harbors in which to ride out a storm. He'd exit at Tamiami, the same as when he turned east for the shelter. This time he would turn west, onto a highway fabled in Florida folklore and preserved in time like a feather in amber.

The city of Miami rises from the last portion of the Florida mainland to emerge from the receding sea during the Pleistocene. Surrounded by water where the Miami River meets Biscayne Bay is a man-made island shaped like a guitar pick. Brickell Key was built from sea bottom dredged from the river's mouth. It's elevation above sea level is three feet and its inhabitants are chiefly white-collar workers making six figures and up. They are hived together in a dense warren of lofty condo towers. The island is connected to the all-the-more affluent mainland Brickell zone by a smallish causeway bridge in view of couples massage suites overlooking the channel from the tony spa at the upper-crust Mandarin Oriental.

The bridge road meets the eastern terminus of the Tamiami Trail, named for its opposite points, Tampa and Miami. U.S. 41 rides piggyback across its length and far beyond to end its northward ascent near a lighthouse on the uppermost Yooper outpost of inhabited Michigan. In Miami it divides as 8th Street east and 7th traveling west. Westbound it threads the heart of Miami's and Florida's Financial Center with its Bruno Magli and Saks and high-hat restaurants amidst soaring towers with penthouses peopled by the fanciest of the schmancy. 7th Street leaves downtown beneath I-95, the

elevated line of demarcation separating Cosmopolitan
Lower Miami from Cuban Miami. West through Little
Havana it passes a block from monuments to Cuban
patriots, sidewalk stars of Cuban pop legends and
dozens of cafes broadcasting aromas of baking
empanadas and strong, sweet cafecito. Past 25th Avenue
7th descends to join Calle Ocho as it glides past the
celebrated Versailles Bakery, of which it is said it that if
you have been to Cuban Miami and have not been to
Versailles, you are under a delusion you have been to
Cuban Miami. Onward, past the Monument to Jose
Marti, Calle Ocho translates back to 8th Street,
advancing past fancy-Dan Coral Gables and the Ritzy
Biltmore. Further still, past the National Hurricane
Center the old road plunges into sixty miles of
Everglades.

It was here that Milo quit the Turnpike and changed
course west onto the East Trail. Tamiami's section
tracing the north border of Everglades National Park
was called the East Trail to distinguish it as the eighty-
mile portion of the road that turns sharply toward the
Atlantic after a 200-mile straight drop down the west
coast from Tampa. He could have taken the direct shot
across the interior on Alligator Alley farther north; a
four-lane ninety-mile straightaway with rest stops. But
he liked the up-close feel of prehistoric Florida that still
inhabited the diminished wild wetlands that remain from
a vanished natural kingdom of sloughs, fens, bogs,
sawgrass marshes and hardwood hammocks. Despite a
century of enduring assault and insult by generations of
dredgers, drainers and developers, The Glades remained
surpassingly benevolent, gifting the bottom of Florida

with storm clouds engorged from the evaporating vastness that painted the vegetation green between the coasts. The sign on the interchange pointing to the Hurricane Center reminded Milo to call up a news station. Healey's shipped to America had no radios, which were installed after-market by dealerships. Milo's was AM only. And the speaker was small and tinny and more suited to news and talk than music. It informed that the latest update had Maxine barely a category one moving unvaryingly northwest in a straight line toward the uppermost Leewards. And the experts agreed that wind shear would foil Maxine's ambitions to play in the majors. Her track would find her in the Middle Keys Friday, but this day was hot and cloudless. A few miles west of the turnpike Milo pulled into the parking lot of the Miccosukee tribal gaming resort. Here, with its two thousand slots, the remnants of the Miccosukee exact lucrative revenge for the Florida Indian Wars upon the white-eyes daily. Danny parked beside him and transferred her bag to the Healey's back seat. Back on Route 41 the lowering sun backlit the tops of slash pines as Milo upshifted cleanly and the veil of nightfall began to overspread the Glades.

"You have a nice car," said Danny, just to say something. She touched the lacquered glovebox of burled walnut and ran her hand across it.

"Thanks. I think of it as proof I can maintain a long-term relationship," replied Milo, aware of sun-tinged skin on a bare shoulder almost touching his own.

In awkward silence Milo tried to focus on the road ahead, his peripheral vision catching flashes of ear and throat at intervals contingent upon the movement of wind-tousled hair.

At length, Danny said, "The Miccosukee took on the name Trail Indians when they gathered along this part of the road when it was built in the '20s. They were a branch of the bloodline of the Seminole and the family tree of both began in the Creek Confederacy up north of the Florida-Georgia line before there was a line."

"You sound as if you know a bit about it," said Milo, interested.

"Anthropology major at UF. I hoped to make a living as a cultural anthropologist with some archaeology crossover. I still do."

"So why aren't you out somewhere working with a pickaxe and a brush?"

"Because I still owe the government a ton of money. The newspaper work pays the bills, and slowly, very slowly, pays off my student loans. Unless you are a Harvard grad recruited to work by the Smithsonian or doing field work underwritten by some dot-com hobbyist billionaire fan of Indiana Jones, starting pay for a neophyte anthropologist is somewhere south of wearing a headset to hear food orders hollered into a drive-through clown face."

Milo smiled. "But as a fellow member of the sub-tropical Fourth Estate, it occurs to me you could have aimed higher in your choice of an interim profession, given that it is well known reporters in Florida are paid in sunshine."

"I've done worse. In Miami-Dade anybody can get a job in telemarketing. But not everybody can write. And not everybody is bilingual. And working at the paper cuts expenses because I can live at home with my mom. I know," she smiled ruefully, "Pretty pathetic."

Milo thought about it. "Why anthropology, if it means you take a vow of poverty?"

Danny turned her face toward Milo's so her words weren't carried away by the rushing wind. "When I was in high school I joined a field trip to Windover over a summer break. You know Windover?"

"I've read something about it. A peat bog?"

A gust carried errant strands of Danny's hair across her cheek to the edge of her mouth and she brushed them away behind her ear.

"Windover's one of the most important archeological sites in the world because bacteria can't live in a peat bog. When ancient people died and their bodies were covered with the peat the skeletons and even the skin and internal organs were perfectly preserved. Eight thousand years. They found intact brains. They even sequenced viable DNA."

"I've covered stories on some other sites," Milo remarked. "The Miami Circle. That big to-do when the state had to pay a developer 26 million dollars to save two dozen holes cut into bedrock."

"Florida has dynamite archaeology. You ask me why anthropology? There's this other peat bog in Central Florida. A cattle ranch. Sixty miles south of Disney. Workers pulled up a man out of the peat a while back. His age was around twenty. He lived in Florida before the time of the classic Greeks, before the Persians, before the Maya. Before the Pyramids. When Ponce de Leon stuck his flag in the sand and gave a Spanish name to a place that had been visited by explorers before him, this young man had already been in the ground way longer than seven thousand years. The anthropologists didn't give him a cute nickname like they used to. They knew he had a name already. They just didn't know it. Old bones get respect. And we don't know everything about him but we know the most important thing. We know that eight thousand years ago, when he died, other people dressed him and placed him gently into the peat and arranged him just so. So we know that eight thousand years ago, someone cared about him. And they still do. He was reburied privately in consultation with Florida tribal officials. That's why I want to do this work."

She has a flair for storytelling, thought Milo. "You know, I think that sort of pre-history detective work is not unlike our mission in Fort Myers. Time traveling to find what is there to find."

Unlike Alligator Alley, Tamiami remains a single lane of asphalt in each direction and has no fences to keep wildlife from crossing, as it will. And wildlife includes forty species of mosquitoes. Milo was aware, as he passed the Ochopee Post Office, the size and shape of a back yard garden shed, that he was, as the crow flies, forty miles above the Florida Bay town of Flamingo. Nicknamed the mosquito capitol of America, swarms there have been sufficiently thick to suffocate livestock. He touched a phone link to a bulletin posted daily by a ranger station displaying the current Everglades mosquito forecast. It displayed the word *extreme* in all-caps. Cruising at speed kept the biters at bay, but Milo was aware he was approaching the Carnestown junction, and should he draw the red light in a fully illuminated intersection the car would be swarmed in seconds. Seeing no traffic ahead or behind he turned off his headlights in the faint glow of moonlight and glided to a stop on the grassy shoulder. In less than a minute he raised the ragtop and rolled up the windows. Fortune smiled and Milo zipped past the Glades Chamber Welcome Center and the gas station (which together comprised the totality of Metropolitan Carnestown) on green as Route 41 began its climb to Naples and Fort Myers.

Danny raised her seatback. She had been reclining so as to observe the night sky. She marveled at the stars radiant in the coal black. This expanse of the Glades was so dark the universe jumped out to surprise the newcomer with how close it was. With the top raised she spoke again. "Granted Florida journalism jobs pay in beach sand. So how do you drive a cool old car and live in a brand new condo in one of the most expensive patches of real estate in the state?"

Milo fished his memory for the best place to begin.

"You remember W.C. Fields said his tombstone would read—All Things Considered, I'd rather be in Philadelphia. Well, that's because he was from Philadelphia and that was a joke. I lived in Philadelphia and I get the joke. Philly's the choice if the alternative is death. Sure, tourists come there because of, you know, Rocky and liberty and cheese-steak. But that's summer."

He had told the story so often it had become a memorized monologue in the script of his life. It was twenty-four years ago that Milo slogged across the Pennsylvania Turnpike in a January snowstorm on assignment for the Philadelphia Enquirer. The paper

christened it The Great Blizzard of 1996. It summoned,
devoid of nostalgia, memories of the Great Blizzard of
1994 and the Great Blizzard of 1993. He'd grown bone-
weary of Paul Bunyan winters where words froze in the
air and had to be gathered up like cordwood and burned
in the fireplace to hear what was said. As he approached
the Breezewood interchange the tropical fragrance of a
Jimmy Buffett song leaked from his radio and, in that
instant, Milo threw caution to the low-visibility wind-
chill. He turned the nose of his car south on 70 toward
where he imagined awaited Margaritaville and where his
Austin Healey could claim its birthright as a convertible.
His car slowed its southward plunge only when it passed
a sign bearing the words, Monroe County; a county
endowed with scenic allure ludicrously more appealing
to Milo than Berks or Schuylkill.

Danny was a good listener, and interjected only to
encourage Milo to carry on when he halted
apologetically; scolding himself for rambling. He carried
on.

Two days after arriving in Key West he combined a
windfall of a journalism cash prize with his nest egg
savings to buy an eighty-five thousand dollar 1928
handyman's special under a shady canopy of live oak on
a lot on Ashe Street with enough room for the boat he
would never buy. With three-quarters down, the bank
was tickled to loan him the rest. By degrees, two
decades of intermittent upgrades later, the ceaseless
hand-to-hand, house-to-house combat among desperate
bidders had placed an eight hundred thousand price tag
on his home. As measured by property value in each of
the last four years his house had earned more income

than he had. His pal Mack had clued him in on the trick to cashing out without becoming homeless in a town where jacking up house prices was a blood sport. Mack knew investor friends who paid nearly a million dollars for a vintage post-and-beam Conch house of Dade County pine and gutted it to create four condos. From the street it remained a vintage post-and-beam Conch house of Dade County pine, encircled by a covered porch sheltered among a crimson sunshade of Royal Poinciana. Within, it was divided into four separate brand new homes. Milo's corner was street side with a porch swing and Adirondack chairs. Milo paid three hundred eighty thousand cash and even factoring assessments he banked four hundred thousand on the old place. The condo was a third the size of his house, but sufficient, and the four owners shared a pool.

Said Milo. "Once your house is paid for, expensive Key West isn't so expensive. I can walk to Schooner Wharf where at seven in the morning happy hour prices are two dollars for domestic draft and an egg and cheese sandwich is under seven bucks." He grinned. "Living my best life."

Chapter 9

Tuesday, April 23, 1929.

It was the best of times. It was the invest of times.
Americans were prospering and stock crazy. The market
had been borne aloft as if by helium for nine straight
years, and since 1922 the Dow had risen 400 percent.
Rags to riches stories of stock successes persuaded
armies of lunchbox-toting average Joes to go into debt
up to their eyeballs to buy stocks. It was common for
rank and file investors to be in hock for 60 to 90 percent
of the face value of all the stock they owned. More
money was on loan than currency in actual circulation.
Wall Street wagering had paid off for so long that
speculation grew white hot and that heat inflated a large
and distended bubble. The Dow Jones reached its acme
at a height of 381 in early September. The flat-out
deflation of the bubble would arrive three summers later
when the Dow hit bottom at 41. But Edison's ad men
were not clairvoyant and in early 1929 Americans were
buying. Buying cars, buying houses and, most

importantly for the men gathered in the third floor photo department on an April afternoon at the Thomas A. Edison Inc. West Orange Building Five, they were buying records. Not Edison Records, however, which was the point of the meeting.

They had pushed together a pair of worn, hard-used oak tables and ringed them with a hodgepodge of mismatched Windsor chairs.

The men chattered amiably about the departmental outing the following day. Brooklyn hadn't won a game in five outings this season and tomorrow Edison, Inc. had organized a jaunt into the city to cheer against the Braves at Ebbets, where their first meeting of the home stand was already under way. Boston had beaten the Robins in the first three away games and hopes were high for payback at home. The marketing team was still expected to punch in for a few hours in the morning before a company bus carried them to the stadium. Several voiced faith in tomorrow's starting pitcher. Jumbo Elliot was six foot five and at two hundred and thirty-five pounds lived up to his name.

Meeting recording secretary Grady Piper opened his notebook and wrote the date. Those near him ribbed him for the hundredth time about the irony that the recording secretary of a company that manufactured recording devices and business dictation machines still took notes on paper with a pencil.

Mort Hall started the meeting with a reminder that today's mission was to regain the market domination Edison Records customarily enjoyed when cylinders were king. The flat disc apostates had won the hearts and minds of a misguided public and the old man had, at long last and grudgingly, embraced a "Can't lick 'em—join 'em" game plan. Or, as Mort characterized it, the "Fuck 'em all" plan.

Several months prior it was decided Edison Records would produce lateral-cut needle-type discs for playing on machines whose rate of rotation was the 78 rpm that had been the standard of motorized phonographs for two decades. Edison was in the process of moving its Manhattan electronic recording studios to a new state-of-the-art facility on Fifth Avenue and engineers had entreated Edison to launch a huge promotional effort because they were convinced the audio quality of their new records was superior to anything produced by competitors. The launch of the new records was set for August and the marketing department was tasked with convincing buyers to come back to Edison for a listen.

Mort was tall and slender with a meticulously groomed full mustache and was otherwise clean-shaven. In public speaking his was an astringent and stiff-necked rhetorical delivery, which suited him as a Presbyterian deacon but oft times miscarried among the back-slapping gang of ad men. He generally wore a checkered suit coat, but it was a warm afternoon and he was in shirtsleeves. He rose and hooked a thumb around a striped suspender. From the back of his throat he sent forth a guttural growl to command attention and called upon the team's sloganeer laureate, Ned Laskey, to present his vision. Mort sat. Ned arose.

"As most are aware, 1929 is a nexus and conjointment of several milestones along the Edison legend timeline." Ned had lots of dandy words. "It was sixty years ago that Mr. Edison arrived in New York

City to begin inventing and commenced work on his
Universal Stock Ticker technology—the triumph that
built Menlo." He paused to scan the nodding faces of
certain colleagues who had shared long hours at Menlo.
Ned bore a marked resemblance to the new American
president, who had taken office the week before. He
underscored the likeness by parting his hair in the
manner of Hoover. His neck, like the president's, was
encircled by a tall and stiff rounded club collar studded
to his starched shirt beneath a tightly-knotted Windsor,
the tie disappearing within a high-buttoned dark vest.
All others present had long ago embraced the current
fashion of soft shirts with collars attached. Ned said, "It
is no secret that the fiftieth anniversary of the
incandescent light will be celebrated in October. As it
affects our phonograph efforts it means the name of
Edison will be lit large this entire Jubilee year. Atlantic
City has big plans for a tribute in June. It is also the
fortieth anniversary of the commercial launch of the
Edison entertainment cylinder that played music and
comic recitations in saloons. So, in addition to the light
Jubilee, that ties together two Edison connections to
current consumer demands: records for home
entertainment and the current bull market in stocks."
Others present responded with approving murmuration
and Ned raised his hand for quiet. "Thirdly, to create
excitement, Mr. Edison has directed that the introduction
of the new discs be celebrated with a promotional stunt
to stimulate sales. Mr. Edison is famously a voracious
reader and keen on Robert Louis Stevenson." Some staff
at the table nodded in agreement as they recalled
carrying out the design of posters when Edison Pictures

made the film of the author's book *Kidnapped.*
"*Treasure Island* had been one of his favorite stories and
the idea of hunting buried treasure fired his imagination.
Also, since Mr. Edison always seeks to ascertain swings
in which of the popular entertainments are in vogue for
business opportunities, he observes that since the first
motion picture of the *Treasure Island* story was released
in 1920, there have been two dozen popular pirate
pictures. Pirates and treasure are popular and the boss
wants a treasure hunt!"

Ned yielded back to Mort, who continued, "Mr.
Edison's home in Florida is several hours sailing from
the Dry Tortugas. Those islands are spoken of in
Treasure Island. Initially, Mr. Edison conceived of
burying a treasure chest on an island in the Tortuga
chain and of revealing clues that would lead searchers to
a Key West schooner that would take them to the island.
I parlayed with accounting and took a meeting with
Charles, who interceded, and together we persuaded his
father that the logistics were impracticable and
impossibly costly. So Dougal will see to the
concealment of the prize at a site that is more accessible.
We've created a rough draft plan to publicize the hunt
and your job will be to refine it for publishing and in-
store displays."

Dougal Brogan was a traveling envoy tasked with
arousing enthusiasm among sales staff in far-flung
outposts and fetching back to the home office customer
assessments of Edison products. As he was the emissary
to the outside, he also carried out the occasional odd job
in transit. He stood and read from a clipboard. "The
grand prize will be stock certificates with a combined

worth of round about twice the yearly income of the average family. Mr. Edison will include shares of T.A.E. Inc. and has secured stock donations from his friends Mr. Ford and Mr. Firestone. Some of you who go back to the early days will remember when we consulted on the electrification of textile mills in New Bedford. Horatio Hathaway expressed gratitude to Mr. Edison for his help with the engines and dynamos with a gift of a number of shares of Hathaway Manufacturing. A portion of those stocks will be added to the others."

Mort broke in. "Whilst we vetoed the Tortugas leg of the hunt, Mr. Edison persuaded us that there could be an advantage of economy by concealing what he calls the treasure chest near Key West."

Dougal nodded, lowered the clipboard and returned his reading spectacles to his vest pocket. "Cost-free transportation by rail will be essential to providing the contestants with the means to travel to the treasure's locality from anywhere. Mr. Edison has cultivated a close relationship with the Florida East Coast Railway in the years since his great friend Flagler commissioned him to light his hotel in St. Augustine. Even after Flagler's death the railroad has furnished Mr. Edison with a private car when requested. I asked a favor and the FEC made an accommodation to assist in tucking away a parcel in a ready-made hollow not in current use by the railway. In this section of tracks the right of way spans 50 feet and I have found a suitable place of concealment near the outermost boundary of a line 25 feet from the track centerline. I did not disclose the contents of the parcel to the railroad. The fewer that know the location and value of the cache the better.

Other than me, only the Edisons—father and son—Ned
and one or two others in the printing department will be
aware of all particulars. I will secrete the package in
September and the contest will be made public in
October to promote record sales in the Christmas season.
And that's Ned's bailiwick."

Ned stepped to a wall-facing easel and turned it
around to reveal a poster bearing the illustration of a
wooden chest. On its side was emblazoned a skull above
crossed cutlasses. Below that image and above a sketch
and signature of Edison appeared the ad copy. "*FIND
YOUR FORTUNE WITH EDISON RECORDS*. The
inventor of aural recording has topped himself with a
new way of producing the best quality sound in all the
world. To celebrate, Mr. Edison and some famous
friends have donated *VALUABLE STOCK
CERTIFICATES* as the hidden *GRAND PRIZE* of a
fortune hunt contest. Hidden among Edison records in
stores everywhere are special messages recorded by Mr.
Edison in his own voice providing clues to the location
of the *TREASURE TROVE*. Follow clues and the
fortunate finder of the *GRAND PRIZE* will be in
clover!"

Ned waited till everyone had examined the mockup.
"I have procured an agreement with the passenger rails
that they will honor travel vouchers included with the
prize recordings and will bill us at a rate of two cents per
passenger mile. This will work in the same way we are
furnishing the students in the scholarship contest with
round-trip rail to West Orange. This new promotion will
raise awareness of the superiority of the new needle-cut
recordings, but we will also press the recordings of Mr.

Edison reading the clues onto Diamond Discs and Amberols so as to reach customers using all players. Dougal has given me his notes as to the precise location of the hiding place and I will compose the clues directing contestants to its discovery. Mr. Edison has directed me to make the effort challenging."

This produced a smattering of chuckles. Edison had created a hiring test to weed out applicants unsuitable for employment at the labs. It contained 146 questions so random (What ingredients are in the best white paint?) that failed job-seekers complained to the newspapers about what the press called "The Impossible Quiz." Reporters challenged celebrities to take the test and Albert Einstein failed it. He could not recall the speed of sound off the top of his head. A wag at the table whispered that if the old man wrote the clues the stocks were safe from discovery. Ned waited for the hilarity to pass and continued.

"We will substitute contest records for various recordings in all categories including popular, jazz, orchestral, opera and spoken entertainment. Ten in total. The boxes will include a railway voucher, spending money for food and such, a key and instructions. Retailers will persuade patrons the more records they buy, the better chance they will have of discovering a special prize recording. In addition to the opportunity to seek out the grand prize, everyone who finds these recordings will receive a new Edison Phonograph and a collection of the new records. The first hunter to solve the clues and find the stock certificates can sell them if he or she chooses. As the shares have been provided from the donors' own securities, it is their expectation they will recover them by buying them back at a premium. But as a legal matter these are bearer shares and will be the property of the holder."

Assignments were handed out and the meeting adjourned with further idle exchanges concerning baseball. Some were looking forward to an extended meeting of the Robins against the Giants at the Polo Grounds where a novel system of electrical loudspeakers had been installed as a new innovation. Even baseball could embrace the electrical epoch. One pragmatist allowed as how the Yankees would likely win it all. They'd reached the Series three years straight and last season swept the Cardinals four straight.

Chapter 10

The Edison winter home and next-door Henry Ford bungalow have earned their keep for seven decades employed as reliable tourist magnets in the *City of Palms*. Fort Myers was hardly a city and on the whole barren of palms when Thomas Edison paid out of pocket for more than a thousand towering royal palm trees. Shipped from Cuba, they were meant as neighborhood decorations lining the lane to the honeymoon haven the widowed inventor built for his new young bride. A new bride who expressed contempt for the putrid stench of this backwater cow town and its odious inhabitants. When Edison's royal palms were neglected by town fathers and died, he charitably had them replaced. At last locals took on the care and feeding of the palms and young Mrs. Edison championed the beautification of her increasingly less-detestable tropical domain. Eventually Mina Edison would love her Florida gardens to the degree she was disinclined to return to her twenty-three-room New Jersey mansion at the end of season. When digital-age marketing consultants floated the idea of replacing *City of Palms* with a fresh nickname, the proposal was roundly vilified on social media and soundly hooted down.

Milo parked in the museum lot, nearly half-filled despite the early hour. Following hours of breezy and exploratory conversation there had been a perfunctory parting after check-in the night before and a quick coffee and bagel in the hotel lobby before pushing off for the Edison home.

The sultry breeze infused the fragrances of the adjacent garden center with a whisper of sea spray from the miles-distant Gulf, and Milo also detected the scent of a big story. It wasn't the first time he'd experienced that big story smell. Most stories grew from seeds planted in press releases and wire copy and rewrites from the morning paper. This story was growing organically and whatever it turned out to be, it was his.

Danny wore the yellow jacket in which she had first appeared at his door. She was luminous in the morning sun. Milo presumed, wistfully, that he was too old for her. They followed the walkway to the welcome center, past a banyan tree of Brobdingnagian enormity.

Danny reached into a small purse and took out a note pad. She said, "I hope we get something useful here. I mean, I hope you don't leave empty-handed after coming all this way. We could have asked the same questions over the phone."

"Says the print media," retorted Milo. "In my racket the craft is judged by the quality of the audio, and listeners know when you're phoning it in. When you stick a nifty yet intimidating ten-inch professional-grade omnidirectional matte-black aluminum XLR microphone in somebody's face the audience intuits that you are going the extra mile, boots on the ground, carrying the station mic-flag into battle, their Murrow in the London Blitz." Milo raised an arm to salute a bigger-than-life sculpture of Thomas Edison as he passed by. "Or," he said, "another way to look at it is that, hey, it's a holiday and the weather is nice and I'm at a pretty place with a pretty woman."

She smiled. "So whose face are you here to stick?"

"Randall Edwards, our contact. I'm not sure what his title is but he's the guy that drew the short straw to work today."

The ticket seller handed Milo an envelope bearing his name containing a pass and without a fuss provided another to Danny. The woman took a moment to unfold an estate map. She marked a dot where the media staffer could be found behind the guest house near the river.

Edwards was supervising a catering crew draping paper runners across folding tables inside a white canvas tent filling a grassy expanse of lawn. Other workers unloaded folding chairs from a truck parked behind the Ford cottage. Extending his hand, he said, "We're hosting a group of travel influencers today. You're welcome at the lunch buffet if you can stick around."

He was puffy and round with short thick curly hair stiff as a Brillo pad, and radiated the enthusiasm of a second-string staffer aware his performance is under constant scrutiny. Perspiring in the swelter of late summer, he extended his hand and his smile faded for a moment.

"Bad business, what happened. Can't wrap my head around it. Those recordings aren't rare. I have a list of them. Let's go to the office. It's a bit of a hike."

With Randall in the lead they trooped from the tent to a riverside pathway hugging the sweeping shoreline of the estate. They passed a grove of bamboo and a variety of trees and shrubs identified by name plates as natives of faraway lands from Mexico to Malaysia. He explained that many had come from Edison's agents in the remote outposts of Edison's years-long research; hunting a botanical source of rubber he could adapt for growing on an industrial scale, a bright idea that fizzled with the invention of synthetic rubber. Together they walked past the guest house, one of two large homes side by side. They were connected by a concrete walkway framed by a wooden pergola decorated by the trellised papery blossoms of a climbing Queen's Wreath. Danny judged the home's composition as Queen Anne-style, despite Queen Anne having moldered beneath Westminster Abbey for more than sixty years before the American colonies declared independence. Victoria reigned when the house was built, but architecture between 1880 and 1910 was called Queen Anne Revival, describing steep roofs and gables and dormers and bay windows. From a long-ago family visit she remembered Edison himself had helped design it, and omitted the front corner tower with a conical roof and most of the other grandiose and showy Queen Anne vernacular. It was plain and simple, like the Midwest-born scientist, but included the requisite vast wraparound porches and spindlework trim.

Randall gestured toward a shady expanse of lawn behind the Edison residence. He said, "This is where Tom and Billie, he called his wife Billie, sat with coffee in the morning watching the birds. They were great bird lovers. Especially Mina. Although her love wasn't all-inclusive. She had her hired man shoot the shrikes that bullied her favorite songbirds." He turned to face his guests and added, earnestly, "Those were different times."

Danny spoke. "How in the world did the Edisons find their way here? This part of Florida must have been really off the beaten track a hundred years ago."

"Longer than that. And yes, it was." Edwards slipped into tour guide mode.

"Local charter captains say the first non-Indian to catch a tarpon in Florida caught it right out there in the Caloosahatchee in 1885. That's the same year Thomas Edison came down and bought this property. He liked to fish tarpon, too. They're a tough fighting fish. They shine like chrome and strike hard and play tug of war in the air. It's a good day when it doesn't dance its way off the line. Gotta let 'em go 'cause they taste like crap. I find 'em revolting, actually. Vile smelling too. All skin and bones. Edison had an electric boat that puttered up and down the river. He preferred river fishing because he got queasy in the Gulf chop." He gestured toward the broad Caloosahatchee and pointed toward the distant shore. "By the way, here's an example of how persuasive the wife of Thomas Edison could be. Mina wrote to the Commissioner of Fisheries at the Commerce Department in Washington and a U.S. Senator asking that fish be stocked in the streams across the river from this house so her husband would have better fishing in the river. And the fish arrived as requested."

Edwards turned away from the river onto the walk leading to the street side of the estate and the visitor's center beyond. He detoured around it through the parking lot and the trio paraded down a road passing between what he pointed out were Edison's research gardens.

"We just passed the botanical lab where the rubber experiments happened. But Edison had an electrical lab next to his house where he could continue working on stuff he had begun in West Orange. That was the one Henry Ford dismantled and took away to Greenfield Village. When Fort Myers town fathers found out about the plan they were apoplectic. They wrote to Edison and pleaded with him to reconsider, calling the lab the crown jewel of the local Edison legacy, not to mention a major tourist draw. Edison told them to talk to Ford. Ford told them to go pound sand."

Their walk ended at a public street at the east gate of the property. Here, a plain single-story home painted white with green shutters had been converted into administrative offices.

Inside, Randall invited Milo to be seated at his desk and presented the printout inventory of cylinders. "Most of those that were stolen are Blue Amberols. That's the name for the hard surface of the record into which the grooves were cut. It was the last improvement in the durability of the records before the business was abandoned. Blue Amberols were chemically an early plastic." He stepped to a shelf on his office wall and

plucked a cylinder from among several on display. He
handed it to Danny. It was an iridescent dark blue and
not much larger than a toilet paper tube. On one end was
etched in white letters, "*K-K-K-Katy*. Billy Murray.
3498." "The catalogue number," said Randall. She
brushed her fingers across the grooves.

"It was the 1920s when this was made, so a goodly
number were jazz. Edison hated jazz. His taste was more
sentimental ballads. And square dances. And patriotic
tunes. John Phillip Sousa believed Edison's phonograph
would destroy the live music business. Why pay to see a
Sousa Band concert if you could hear it anytime at
home? For a long time he refused to be recorded. But
once he saw how good the money was, his band became
the first pop supergroup. But as to jazz, there was a good
one in this bunch called *I Love College Girls*. By Earl
Oliver's Jazz Babies. A solid band. Here's a fox trot
called *Roll 'Em Girls* by the Florida Four. That was
about the flapper fad of women rolling their stockings
down below the knee. We try to mix it up with the
records we loan out for exhibits. So there were some
World War One songs in those boxes. A 1918 tune
called *If He Can Fight Like He Can Love, Goodnight
Germany!* Some songs about Prohibition. They were
usually funny. Like this one. *It's the Smart Little Feller
Who Stocked Up His Cellar that's Getting the Beautiful
Girls*."

Milo handed a page to Danny. "To your question.
There are some Latin titles here."

Edwards nodded. "Yes, there was an entire Blue
Amberol Mexican series. And a Cuban series."

Milo ran a finger down the titles and paused. "And what would you call this series? *Massa's in De Cold, Cold Ground. Hear the Pickaninny Band. Roll Them Cotton Bales. A Darkey's Oration on Women.*"

Edwards was conditioned by his employment to defend the Edison brand. "Those were different times," he said again. "There were still people alive who fought in the Civil War. Jolson was still doing blackface."

Milo came to the end of the list. "If there's anything in these titles that suggests a motive for murder I can't see it."

"Me neither," said Edwards. "Nothing you couldn't buy on eBay for a few dollars."

Milo switched gears. He'd decided he could talk around the subject of the contest without revealing his purpose. "Somebody suggested I ask about any significance you might attach to a group of four names. Edison, Ford, Firestone and Hathaway. Don't think about each name. Just all four together. Anything?"

Edwards raised his face to the ceiling, chin out, brows narrowed and was silent for a moment. "Not immediately. Of course I know a lot about the first three. But I can't say I've seen those four names together in any context. But now I've got to excuse myself. I have to check on the reception for the travel group. Their bus is due. We can talk again after lunch if you wish. Let's walk and talk and maybe something will occur to me."

Milo pulled out a microphone and held it beneath Edward's face as they retraced their steps toward the estates. It caused him to refocus. "Let me tell you a little of what I know about three names. I may have an idea about the fourth. Edison and Ford were chummy in the

extreme. Ford worked for Edison as chief engineer at
Edison Electric in Detroit before his boss advised him to
chase his car dream. Edison was his Yoda mentor. Some
might call it a bro-mance but I'd say it was more like
Ford was an Edison fanboy. They camped out together.
They traveled on business together. And at the end Ford
bought up two of Edison's landmark invention labs and
put them in his personal museum with no beaker out of
place. He was the world's most fanatical Edison
memorabilia collector, and his collection included
Edison himself. They were birds of a feather as nobody
in the country was more famous than either of them.
Ford bought the house next door here. He and Edison
founded the local country club and Edison served on the
board. First golf course on the Gulf coast. Just a mile
from here. They were golfing buddies. They were
fishing buddies." Edwards paused to toss a fallen
coconut to the side of the road. "Now comes Harvey
Firestone. He makes tires in Akron but so does
Goodyear and General Tire and BF Goodrich. But
Firestone sucks up to Ford and brownnoses his way into
the Gilded Age robber baron fraternity. Ford puts
Firestone tires exclusively on all his cars and Harvey is
on the gravy train. But the price of knowing the secret
handshake in the Gilded Age robber baron fraternity is
being stuck in the role of Henry Ford's valet. An
enormously well-paid valet, but still a yes-man. Sure he
can go on the camping trips as long as he organizes them
and acquires all the supplies. Ford and Edison just have
to show up. So Edison and Ford lived here. Harvey
stayed in the guest house when he visited his BFFs.
Some of the most famous people in America stayed in

the guest house." Edwards stopped and faced Milo. "As a reporter, you can appreciate this. Everything that happened here was reported nationally. Being a guest of Edison's made you a player in those years. Your name and photograph might appear beside his in society blurbs in the Sunday rotogravures. If the fourth name was Hoover instead of Hathaway I'd have had it. Herbert Hoover came here when he was president-elect in 1929 to celebrate Edison's 82nd birthday along with Ford and Firestone." The trio resumed its hike.

"Any light bulbs go off yet about Hathaway?"

"No. Sorry. But let me finish up about the other three and I'll make a suggestion. So Harvey Firestone liked Florida as much as the others. He lived seven years past Edison and died at his own vacation house on Miami Beach. And the Firestone and Ford bloodlines literally merged. Harvey's son Harvey Jr. took over the company and he had four kids. One of them was the original Harvey's granddaughter Martha. She married William Clay Ford, the youngest grandson of Henry Ford. They were fixed up by their mothers. William was on the board at Ford for fifty-seven years and when he died his boy William Clay Jr. became CEO and is now chairman of the Board. He personally owned almost seven million shares of Class B stock and twenty-six million common shares, making him the largest stockholder in the company. When William Sr. died in 2014, Martha, the Firestone granddaughter, inherited a ton of cash and the Detroit Lions. She was ninety-four when she gave the team to her daughter. So that's the three names I know. I can call those up in my own head. But we have a computer with its own archives search engine and a lot of Edison documents to search. The Edison stuff from here is small compared to the trainload up in the old West Orange labs. Mostly hand-written letters between Mina and her kids and relatives. But there were some lab notebooks and loose notes and business papers saved after Edison died. And a collection of minutes taken at company meetings. Stuff like that." They arrived back at the parking lot and Edwards waved at a group stepping out of a bus. He turned back to Milo and Danny.

"Our IT guy is off today. But we have a contractor finishing up his work on the system right now and he's got to be gone tomorrow. There's the welcome center. Ask at the desk for Griff. Griff Cameron. He's usually in the remote office but because it's a holiday and there's nobody to watch him he's wrapping up his work in the museum office. Tell him I sent you. He can search those names together and see if anything pops up."

Edwards strode off with a wave. Milo was hopeful. His inner voices briefly debated denying Danny entry into the computer room, but protecting his competitive edge became moot the moment he'd confirmed she wasn't working a story. Prudence had moved him to phone Diarios Las Americas to verify Danny's CV as the two were driving in tandem across the Seven Mile Bridge. He told an editor he was an employer checking references. The editor had been her supervisor. Daniela Carreras had taken a leave of absence four months back and he was unaware of her plans. Yes, she had done a story about Latin language antique cylinder thefts, "a puff piece, oh, I'd say something more than a year ago." Yes, her work had been very good. He would recommend her. Milo didn't know what her game was,

but "keep enemies closer" seemed to fit the situation.
Was she an enemy? Jury's out. But keeping Daniela
close? It's a thought.

   He seemed genuine, thought Danny, glancing at
Milo. Not bad to look at. Tall and lean and funny.
Smart, too. Sandy hair. Sort of mussed, in a cute way.
Forearms deeply tanned. Doesn't duck the sun. In other
circumstances, she might not reject an invitation for a
drink. But as it was, she knew she would be persona non
grata if he discovered she was a…what was she? I'm a
mole, she decided. She'd phoned cousin Griffin as she
followed the little green sports car across the causeway
to the mainland and said he could expect them in the
morning. She reminded her conscience that she was a
prisoner of circumstances and was not by nature
deceitful. She'd consented to Griff's employment as
office temp as a necessary evil to make headway toward
solvency. He'd given her a phone and paid her to
assume the role of receptionist at *Unfolding Web
Technologies* to give the impression the operation was
more than a one man band. She'd known of his sketchy
history and time spent as a guest of the state, but a career
path that enforcers of social order might construe to be
extralegal had been followed by more than one of her
classmates, and who was she to judge? They were still,
after all, fellow Barracudas.
   When Milo entered the picture Cameron had
persuaded her to get close enough to the reporter to
observe his search for the stocks. If she tipped her
cousin to their location, or confirmed Milo had found

them, he promised she could kiss her student loans goodbye and buy a condo on the water. She tried to unsee his indelicate leer as he growled, "Do what it takes. Whatever you have to do

Chapter 11

Griff had experienced momentarily jitters when he learned of Milo's impulsive dash up Route 41. His mind raced through scenarios in which he had somehow been exposed and his Sherlock puppet-on-a-string was coming to confront him. No. He reassured himself that it was only natural the reporter would wish to visit with the owner of the stolen cylinders. He began devising a stratagem by which he could manipulate this new opportunity to his advantage. Through Gorse he had delivered a clue, but it was apparent Milo needed another piece of the puzzle to provide him a pathway to real progress. A meeting would be an opportunity to further expose his dog to the scent.

Griff had scanned into his computer the old photostats of the Edison marketing meeting synopsis and the accounts statements and reversed the negatives to positive images; more readable and easier on the printer. He copied them into an unnamed desktop folder and returned to his task of wrapping up his unproductive work for the Estates trustees.

The next morning found him again at his computer, Milo and Danny seated across his desk, leaning in, attentive. Milo was dressed comfortably in island casual; his shirt a collarless pullover with sleeves rolled. He observed that notwithstanding the holiday and his job site away from public view, Cameron wore long trousers and a white dress shirt. His only concession to the heat was the absence of a tie. Milo's notes would sketch the man as around forty and fit, with a tall and rectangular-shaped face with a severe pointed chin and what Hollywood publicists called a pencil-thin mustache in the era of Errol Flynn and William Powell. His dark hair was fastidiously styled in a Princeton cut with the part on the left.

"Edison contest 1929," said Griff, typing the words into a search box in an internal museum documents database. "Got a few hits. Some of them are contests for most productive salesmen in various divisions. We'll pass over those. Here's one that made all the papers. Scholarship contest. Like a college bowl quiz. July thirtieth through the second of August at the West Orange lab. Forty-nine boys from the States and DC. Winner was Wilbur Huston, who got a full ride to MIT and went to work for Theo Edison. A note attached says Wilbur later became a rocket scientist. Was Mission Director of the Nimbus weather satellite program at NASA and kept busy in retirement as a computer software consultant. Anyway, when he competed as a high school brainiac in 1929 this says he got his picture taken with Charles Lindbergh. With the other boys he watched Babe Ruth strike out against Cleveland at

Yankee Stadium and ate hot dogs at Coney Island before
being put on the train home."

"Try adding these four names to the search," said
Milo, handing Cameron a scrap of paper. Griff dutifully
entered the names, knowing the documents on which
they appeared together existed in no database. He gave
the appearance of initiating a search and instead
switched screens to display the scanned contest notes.
"This looks interesting. It's a brief summary contained
in a multi-page file but the names are all here. I'll print
it. Also a bookkeeping ledger entry for a contest. You
can judge whether it's of any consequence." The whirr
of the printer drew everyone's attention to the emerging
pages. Milo riffled through them and discarded all save
two. "100 shares each," he said. "The companies are
named for their founders. All four." Griff asked, "This is
helpful?"

Milo stood and reached across the desk for a
handshake. "I think it is. I think it absolutely is."

The return trip south was unremarkable. Confined
together in the small car, Milo undertook to pass the
time with light banter, but Danny's demeanor was
restrained. He remained keenly drawn to her without
knowing anything of substance about her. She was so
close to him but felt out of range. She engaged with him
agreeably enough in superficial conversation, but Milo
picked up a vibe of introspection. He wondered if the
cause was what he sensed shortly before they got back
on the road. He'd thanked the computer consultant for
his time and exited the office to rejoin the media contact

at the lunch buffet. Danny had hung back to ask her own
questions, which raised questions. She'd lied about
being on assignment. So to what purpose was her choice
to linger behind? Was it an illusion that he had sensed
some flash of familiarity between her and Cameron? It
was a baseless hunch, but his gut was seldom far off the
mark. Bird Dog, they'd called him in his newspaper
days. Alerting on a scent gave cause to point, regardless
of whether a prey was flushed. For reasons unknown,
the spark of Danny's passionate enthusiasm on the way
north had been extinguished.

"Here's your car," said Milo, as he braked to a stop in
the casino parking lot. "Hope you got enough to make
the ride worthwhile." Danny opened the passenger door
and reached into the back seat for her bag. She turned
back to face him.

"Look. I don't know if my editor will want anything
more on this thing, but I hope if I turn up again you
won't think I'm a pest. I enjoyed the trip and very much
appreciate your kindness in taking me along. If I don't
see you again, I'll be disappointed."

She closed the door and waved without spirit. Then
she was gone.

Milo felt both beguiled and manipulated. But he also
hoped to see her again. She was quick of wit and
nobody's fool. Even in stillness there resided behind her
tawny eyes a barely concealed uninhibited spontaneity.
And her body was so splendidly organized. Meanwhile,
there was work to be done.

He knew zip about the stock market. He had reported
the current Dow Jones numbers on-air day to day with
the rudimentary understanding they reflected prevailing

investor sentiment. But he owned no stock and never had. Cal would know. He would ask Cal. Another thing. How could a bank account stay active without anybody paying attention over the span of ninety years? Aren't there laws about that? He'd seen ads for outfits that help find unclaimed property. Forgotten tax refunds and pension funds people forgot they paid into. But he had a vague recollection that states collected all those things and coughed up the cash in abandoned accounts only when the owner wised-up and filed a claim. Wouldn't a bank remove an account that nobody had touched since Prohibition? Ben would know. He would ask Ben.

Descending from the mainland onto Key Largo he passed mile marker 105 and remembered that the vanished Key Largo train depot had boarded passengers at marker 105.6. He never forgot this arcane trivia because, by happenstance, 105.6 was the frequency of the radio home from which he'd defected only last week. The thought of cutting ties with K-105 reminded him to deep-six his station email for good. He'd used his new webmail account to distribute media queries. Another gratifying step toward his permanent disengagement from Barry.

His thoughts returned to mile markers. The contemporary mile markers known to tourists climb from zero starting in Key West, but in the railroad's heyday Key West was zero only as a starting line northbound. Southbound trains started at zero in Jacksonville and track's-end in Key West was milepost 522. Each time he descended the Keys it occurred to Milo to regret not having known the excitement of riding the elegant coaches of the overseas line. Before

the hurricane wrecked the railroad one could board a
train in West Palm Beach before five in the morning and
arrive at track's end before noon. If you should fancy an
authentic mojito you could step off the train in Key
West and walk steps across a pier to a waiting steamship
that would deliver you to Havana before seven the same
evening.

Mile markers. Milo recalled the meeting notes
contained in an envelope now residing in his glove box.
He thought, "To which mile marker did the Flagler man
take the Edison man?"

He keyed his earpiece and directed his phone to dial
Cal. Yes, he could meet at the Wharf in the morning.
Yes, he would try to assemble a quorum.

Passing over Tea Table Key Channel onto toothpick-
narrow Indian Key Fill he slowed behind a line of cars
packed with young people convoying into a sandy pull-
off. Milo recalled his oath of tolerance as his mouth
silently formed the words, "Labor Day pestilence."The
Fill was the holiday go-to place for unwelcome day-
tripping mainlanders.

As the road cleared again and he accelerated, Milo
was reminded that there were disadvantages to
remaining in a committed relationship with an old sports
car. He'd bought the roadster at an estate sale when he
was making good money at the paper. Its value had
ballooned like his house and its price tag would be out
of reach now. British racing green. Cockpit enfolded in
leather soft as a catcher's mitt. Polished inlaid walnut
shifter standing at attention ready for duty at his right
hand. He loved the curving bonnet and the baritone
growl of its exhaust. The steering wheel of laminated

mahogany was riveted and burnished to a glossy patina.
Still, there was no air conditioning and the heat radiating
from the engine compartment added another ten degrees
to an already steamy summer's day. The interior was
more than a little claustrophobic for a human of Milo's
beanpole stature. But with the top down and an open
road none of that mattered. The nimble little car could
reach speeds of 120 miles an hour, a level of
performance afforded by zero roads in the Florida Keys.
Still, as its gleaming wire wheels flashed past
pedestrians and other drivers at the posted speed limit,
Milo was accustomed to returning smiles and upraised
thumbs. And women found it so freaking adorable.

Chapter 12

Schooner Wharf Bar was rustic in contrast with the string of stylish waterfront bars and restaurants dotting the periphery of Key West Bight. It was built by mariners to attract mariners and expanded over the years into a patchwork jumble of timbers and tin, infused with the permanent aroma of fried conch and shrimp. The more weathered the gray patina of its planks the more luminously it gleamed as a lighthouse beckoning loyal barflies. It had been contrived to be a dive.

Junie poured Mack a pint of Sunset Ale, set it on the bar and said "So what is it about famous rich men and their trophy wives?"

Junie was tall and tan with legs of a runner, which she was. Her hair was long and blond and tied up in a ponytail. She was probably on the sunny side of thirty and no one was inclined to rub her the wrong way by inquiring. The men at the bar, and more than a few of the women, daydreamed of rubbing her the right way. A year away from an associate's degree in business management from Florida Keys Community College, Junie was pragmatic about her attraction and used it to advantage. She had perfected a bar trick whereby she would slide her eight-inch flat-steel bottle opener from her rear pocket and spin it like a gunfighter in a wild west show. She'd swiftly decapitate the bottle and slide it across the bar as she spun the opener again and turned her hip to provide the customer a display of its re-holstering in the hind pocket of shorts so snug and brief their wearing would draw a week's high school detention, minimum. After two months her spreadsheets noted tips had increased 13%. Some of the older male regulars had switched from draft to bottles.

Milo had just related, in his summary of his Fort Myers reconnaissance, that a thirty-nine year-old Thomas Edison had taken a twenty-year-old bride when they set up housekeeping in Florida.

"Could be that was the usual way of it in those days?" said Millie Mae, reaching for the Eskimo's empty Yeti. Millie Mae was another among legions of winsome young bartenders hired with an eye to keeping tourists bonded like barnacles to their seats. A seasoned hand at bar diplomacy, she was disinclined to observe aloud the illogic in his purchase of an insulated tumbler. The man had never met a drink he didn't finish cold.

Milo said, "All I know is that Edison met his first wife when she was fifteen and they were married three months after she turned sixteen."

Mack said, "George Clooney's wife is seventeen years younger."

Ben said, "And Harrison Ford is twenty-two years older than what's her name? You know. Ally McBeal."

Looking up from his phone Cal said, "Bogie and Bacall? Twenty-five-year gap says Google."

Junie said, "I rest my case."

A new voice growled from down the bar. "Needed him some of that young poontang," said a hunched old man with a whiskered thin face. He nursed a bottle of Corona, an unfiltered cigarette pinched by trembling fingers the color and texture of saddle leather. He'd been listening. "Been the wreck of many a man. So I know to my regret. Yes, sir. The wreck of many a man." No one spoke and presently, self conscious, he turned away.

Milo pressed on. "So the prize was a bunch of stock certificates but the contest never happened. I have a call in to the Edison Factory museum in New Jersey to find out why." But meanwhile it would be good to know, before we agree they were what got Nathan Parker killed, if these certificates are worth more than novelty souvenirs. We know what happened to stocks in 1929."

A phone sounded a bell tone. "End of morning watch," said Mack. The men all arose, took their drinks from the bar and walked the few steps to the boardwalk. They gathered in a line shoulder to shoulder with their faces to the sea beyond the charter fishing boats, the dive boats, the sight-seeing boats, the party boats, the mega-yachts. The cloudless morning sky was the color of faded jeans. After a few moments the music began. It was the raising of the colors on board the Coast Guard station a few hundred yards distant. The all-weather public address speakers blasted the anthem every morning at eight on the dot. They stood with drinks in hand. Ex-army diver Mack was the only one of the bunch with military service and saluted. When the final notes faded, in unison they raised their glasses and took a swallow. They returned to the bar. Mack had started it as a solitary ritual years ago. Over time the rest of the band had joined him. Attendance fluctuated in the breakfast hour, but those who show up stand with the Coasties.

Milo was the youngest of the squad but as a reporter was at home in the company of pensioners. He celebrated Florida as the world's foremost geriatric sanctuary and one of the largest repositories of untapped wisdom. Let others mock the migratory masses of Methuselahs. Milo venerated them as the mother lode of radio features. When stumped for a story he would phone up a retirement home. "Somebody interesting? You gotta meet Paul. Used to be captain of the Presidential Yacht Sequoia. Ask him about that night on the Potomac with Marilyn Monroe." "A good story? Everybody here adores Leo. He plays the ukulele on the bus to Publix. Used to be Ambassador to China."

His bar gang weren't candidates for nursing homes, but in retirement they had all brought to Florida a lifetime's accumulation of expertise and weren't reticent about sharing it. Milo regarded his older pals who were émigrés from the north as risk takers; wagon train pioneers journeying into uncharted territory in their southbound caravan of Chrysler New Yorkers. Refusing to die where they lived, their migration to the Keys was driven less by the discarded snow-blower than by the bold enterprise ahead. Like Joe Cable to Bali Ha'i, they were drawn by the sun to the soft tropical embrace of scented breezes; a destination for introspection. A place to write their own epilogues.

Milo had aspired to step off the treadmill at fifty and had beaten it by two years. Two more years on the sunny far side of work. He was mystified by those who wondered how they could possibly escape boredom in retirement. He could think of a few things. It occurred to him, not for the first time, to resent being duty-bound to move this last ball across the goal line.

Ben said, "So Cal will find out about the stocks and I'll look into the bank account."

Benjamin Cobb retired to Key West after a career as a forensic accountant at a Delaware Law Firm. He did consulting work for the Delaware State Auditor and relished taking the stand and translating the abstruse language of finance into vocabulary comprehensible to a judge and jury. He drew a comfortable pension but supplemented his bar tabs across the island by doing taxes for chums.

"I'd be surprised if an account dormant for so long would have escaped being seized by the state. Either New York, which is where the account is, or by New Jersey where the corporate owner of the securities resided. I'll be better able to mull it over when I hear what Cal digs up."

Cal said, "I'll head out tomorrow." He signaled Junie for a refill. Mack held up two fingers to include himself. Mack drank Key West Sunset Ale because he always supported anything with Key West in the name. It mattered not to him that it was brewed four hundred miles north up Cape Canaveral way.

Milo pressed on. "The sketchy notes in the file also refer to a voice recording made by Edison himself that provides directions to the grand prize. Random record buyers would find the special cylinder in a handful of packages that were switched out. Like Willie Wonka's

golden tickets. And an interesting note records that one
of the Edison team was to meet with the Florida East
Coast Railroad to arrange for placement of the prize
package. I talked with the Flagler Museum in Palm
Beach. They said Edison was connected to Flagler in
several ways. They were friendly business associates.
Scratched each other's backs. Edison lit the first hotel in
the country with electric lights. It was Flagler's Ponce
de Leon in St. Augustine. When the hotel opened its first
guests were so afraid of being electrocuted Henry
Flagler had to hire employees whose job it was to switch
on the room lights. Edison sometimes rode in a private
car provided him by the Florida East Coast Railroad
when he worked in Florida. Eight years later Edison lit
the Southernmost House here. Mrs. Harris, the lady of
the house, was a friend of Edison's. She and her
husband were investors in Flagler's railroad. Also,
Edison tried to pitch Flagler to buy Edison cement to
build the trestle bridges between the Keys."

   At seventy-two, Diego was the oldest member of the
group and island-born. As a third generation Cuban-
Conch his bar mates had bestowed upon him the
honorific "Don." Don Diego's parents had sold the
family café and retired to Tampa where Cubans had
assimilated a half-century before the Castro refugees
brought political activism to Miami. The Don lived in
his childhood home and continued to earn a paycheck
driving a Conch Train and lecturing tourists as a bona
fide sage of local history.

   "My great-grandmother cooked for parties at the
Harrises. The man of the house was Judge Jeptha Vining
Harris and it's easy to remember his family tree because

he was the son of another Jeptha Vining Harris who was a surgeon for the Confederates and became the head Key West Customs officer. One could get quite rich presiding over customs in those days. Dr. Harris had a grandfather and an uncle also named Jeptha Vining Harris. But about his boy the judge? It can be argued that his grandest singular achievement was marrying the richest girl in town."

The Eskimo said, "Why was it that all these rich people moved to Key West?"

With a laugh The Don shook his head.

"That's what's most forgotten about this town. In the middle of the 1800s Key West was the wealthiest town in America and Florida's biggest city. Rich people didn't move here. They got rich here. They sold sponges from here. In winter they sold fruit and vegetables grown here. They sold meat from sea turtles caught and canned here. People up north seasoned their food with Key West sea salt. My relations were brought here to cook for the Cuban cigar rollers. But most got rich two ways. Some were merchants selling or transferring stuff that arrived on docks daily from ships from everywhere. And some waited for those ships to hit rocks and sink and then sold all the stuff they could carry off from the wrecks. But old Bill Curry figured instead of working day and night waiting for a wreck and then quasi-legally looting it lock, stock and deck planks, he could sell the wreckers everything they needed to do their jobs. So he became the richest of all in the marine supply business. He used that money to buy and sell property and some say he was the richest man in Florida."

Milo's phone vibrated. It was a text. Its sender was Detective Sergeant Matthews. "Got your computer. You home?" Milo keyed back, "Give me forty minutes. See you there." He turned back to Don Diego as he concluded his history lesson.

"So Bill Curry had eight kids and made them all rich, too. His boy George built an ice plant and an electric plant providing the fishermen night lights and ice to keep the catch from spoiling. There's a saying Key West was the first city in the state to get electric lights and the last to get indoor toilets. Long story longer Florida had been very, very good to old Bill Curry, so he named his youngest daughter Florida. It was Florida Curry who married Judge Harris and her money built the house that cost a quarter million dollars when a dollar was worth three cents in today's money. She wanted to put space between her and the mansions of her brothers near the seaport so she built her big house on the opposite side of town and hired Edison to light it. Henry Flagler stayed there too when he was in town getting his railroad built."

Junie refreshed glasses and said, "So back to his wives. In that Edison light bulb movie. Was that his first wife or his second wife?"

Cal said, "Which light bulb movie?

"Umm. The black and white one."

Milo said, "Mina wasn't in any of those movies. That was Mary, the first wife. She was Mrs. Edison for the phonograph and the light bulb. She died just before her twenty-ninth birthday. Then a friend fixed him up with Mrs. Edison number two. But even though Mina wasn't in those Edison movies she was his wife when he invented movies. Mina was the daughter of a mega-rich farm machine inventor from Akron. At her wedding, she was only seven years older than her thirteen year-old step-daughter. "

Don Diego said, "Spencer Tracy was good in the movie."

"Who's Spencer Tracy?" asked Millie Mae.

Mack chimed in. "But in that new one? Cumberbatch as Edison? Whose bright idea was that?"

Junie nodded. "I know, right? He made Edison seem like a prick."

Mack said, "I mean, don't get me wrong, nobody doesn't like Cumberbatch. Everybody loves Cumberbatch. We can stipulate he was fine as that English guy who built the code machine to eavesdrop on the Nazis. Probably why he got typecast as an intense and moody genius inventor. But you can't find an intense and moody American actor who can play an intense and moody American genius inventor? Heck, the movie inventor with more patents than Edison is intense and moody Tony Stark." Mack bowed his head. "May he rest in peace."

Junie said, "Maybe it's payback for Downey, Jr. playing Sherlock."

Cal said, "I stick up for Cumberbatch. He was fine. No worse than the movie about Edison as a kid. Mickey Rooney, for cryin' out loud."

"Who's Mickey Rooney?" asked Millie Mae.

His presentation at an end, Milo observed, without engaging in, a debate over which of the bar's offerings was the superior tequila.

He was tempted to shoo away the albatross of commitment and linger. But Jack Matthews was on the way and there were inquiries to make. Milo left the Wharf and started home alongside the marina. In the water below, the gaping mouth of a Goliath Grouper lurked beneath a charter boat awaiting the windfall of a fish-gutting. Formerly called a Jewfish, federal officials, under public pressure, renamed it Goliath, who was not a Jew, but a Philistine, and nobody cares about offending them.

Jack Matthews sat on the porch stairs fiddling with his phone. Milo's laptop was on the step at his feet. They bumped fists. Milo said, "Thanks for the note explaining what the IT guy found. Good idea to leave it to the expert."

"He says the keylogger whatamahickey was probably installed from a flash drive. That's according to Martin. I wouldn't know a keylog from a tree frog. Turns out there are different kinds and this one was a sort of screen grab dealie where somebody could see an image of what you type. Which is why I asked what you wanted done with it?"

Milo momentarily weighed pros and cons of reporting his Fort Myers expedition to Jack. It was about time to be straight with the detective. He awarded con the win. This was not that time.

"Tell Martin thanks for getting rid of it. I thought about leaving it alone and writing misleading stuff to put him or them or whomsoever on the wrong track if I ever come up with a right track. But right now I really need the computer for work."

"At least we know why the guy what jumped you was in the house. No doubt to snoop out what the reporter knows about the murder." Jack's tone made it known he had transmuted from pal to cop. "Which would also be what the police know if the reporter shared what he knows with the police. Like any good citizen would be sure to do." Jack stood and brushed sand off his trousers. He walked to his car at the curb, opened the door and, before he climbed in, locked eyes with Milo and pointed toward the front of the cruiser, "Like it says there on the fender. Protecting and serving paradise. See you around citizen."

Chapter 13

Gorse had arrived in New York Monday night. It was now Wednesday and he hoped to make his red-eye return flight, wheels-up in less than four hours. Of course when Griff's ex-cellmate cyber-security pal completed the favor asked of him, he had to be, as Gorse believed special forces would put it, terminated with extreme prejudice. No getting around it. One can't con a con, and the other man sniffed opportunity the instant he saw the numbers. He had said as much, and pressed Griff to cut him in on whatever hustle this was. Cameron applied flattery with a trowel, giving assurances that his was the first name that came to mind when hunting up a partner possessed of certain skills. He said he would circle back once he'd nailed some things down, and then called Gorse to nail something down.

Gorse thought of himself as a covert operative, and had stalked his objective the day before, stepping from a Lower Manhattan skyscraper elevator on the hunt to find a brokerage firm whose name matched the one Griff had written on a card. The card also bore a man's name, first and last, and his home address. Gorse was gratified to discover the corporate offices were in plain view behind a wall of glass spanning most of the hallway. He dialed the phone number displayed on the door and watched as the receptionist touched a keyboard and spoke into a headset.

"Grissom, Bennett and Heyward. How may I direct your call?" Gorse replied and keenly scanned the several offices that ringed the reception desk, also with walls of glass. There. A man behind a desk lifted a phone and spoke. Gorse saw his mouth move as he said, "Fagan." Gorse hung up and studied the man's face. It was a man of perhaps thirty years and slim wearing an expensive-looking suit of dark gray. The description fit. Gorse disconnected.

Gorse picked the man out of a crowd and followed as he exited the office building in Lower Manhattan and stopped into a bar for an hour, perhaps to wait out the rush as the city emptied. The bartender appeared to know the man and Gorse thought it likely that this stop was part of a daily routine. His mark led him down into the Wall Street Station of the Lexington Line and into a number five subway. He rode north in darkness till the train emerged into dusky daylight above ground in the Bronx. There was no air conditioning and some windows were lowered to half-staff. Into the car flowed a fusion of steel track joint rhythms, gusty wind and traffic noise. Gliding through timeworn neighborhoods stained by varying degrees of decay there were flashes of corner delis, money-wire storefronts, pawn shops and laundromats. He followed the man as he exited the car at Morris Park. Everything in New York City felt confining to Gorse. The big buildings made the sky

small. New York had more than Florida in every
category save space.

The prey descended the stairs from the station and
walked into the neighborhood to its west. Gorse judged
it to be a nice neighborhood. Neat brick homes where
owners had invested time planting flowers in yards and
window boxes. He followed until the man turned the
corner up a cross-street and disappeared into the lobby
of a large red brick apartment building fronting a half-
block. The address matched the one on the card in
Gorse's hand. A sign proclaimed it to be a tower, at
seven stories. Another sign declared it to be luxurious,
with which portrayal Gorse had no basis for dispute.
Gorse had no intention of entering. The exterior was
windows and glass doors and there appeared to be
nothing in the lobby but walls of mailboxes. The room
was brightly lit. Too public.

He retraced the sidewalks to the train station,
scouting for a hunting blind. It was a six minute walk to
the IRT. Likely what sold the man on the apartment.
Gorse required concealment and a place to park a car.
He turned and walked the man's route home. He paused
for a moment to inspect a tall hedge bordering a
sidewalk but hiding behind it would place him in
someone's back yard. He kept walking. He saw
residents sitting on stoops outside, reading or talking on
phones. People still did that? Too much exposure on the
street lined with houses. He turned on to the street filled
with apartment buildings. A vacant lot bordered the
luxury tower. Some construction had begun and the site
was screened with a veil of plywood sheets eight feet
high. One of the panels was fitted with hinges as a door

and secured with an inexpensive padlock. Gorse opened
his map app, tapped current location and sent the GPS
bookmark to himself as a text.

That happened yesterday. Now it was dusk again. He
had arrived early to wait, patiently circling the block for
more than an hour until a parking spot appeared. The
rental was snug against the curb, just steps from the wall
of plywood. Again the site had been undisturbed by
activity and when Gorse was convinced he was unseen
he had snipped off the lock. He tossed the bolt cutter
into the car for later use.

The street lights had come on when the man rounded
the corner from the next street and approached. Gorse
had swung the plywood panel fully open and flat against
the wooden wall, leaving the open space through which
he stepped to grab the man from behind and drag him
struggling backward into the lot while applying the
disabling pressure hold that was his signature. As it did
with Milo, the blockage of the carotid swiftly induced
unconsciousness and when the man was out Gorse
blocked his nose and mouth to suffocate him. He picked
up the man's briefcase and placed it inside the wooden
walls as he swung the door closed, walked calmly to his
car and slipped behind the wheel. He switched on the
radio and scanned till he fixed on WCBS and listened to
the local news. Florida news seemed far less dreadful
when compared to the criminality of New York City.

The dusky light faded to black. The street was silent.
Gorse popped the trunk of the rental and hurried to
swing open the plywood door. He carried the body and
the briefcase to the car. He had reconnoitered early in
the day and had a plan. The object was to deflect

questions about why and how death had come to the
commuter. He needed the body on the tracks but the
nearest station was elevated. Not far away to the north
the tracks were ground level below the Gun Hill Road
Station. The Gun Hill Road Bridge was protected by a
tall metal fence to prevent falls or jumps onto the tracks
below. That fence ended at the junction with an adjacent
street, where only a knee-high concrete wall bordered a
heavily wooded ravine that sloped down to the tracks.
Gorse stopped briefly to toss the body and case over the
short wall into the underbrush and parked a few blocks
away. He walked back warily, alert to trouble and
holding the bolt cutter unobtrusively beside his leg.

Down the wooded embankment he dragged the body
and snipped away some chain link to arrive trackside.
He pulled the body across to the opposite side of the
tracks and into another jumble of trees and brush. He
retrieved the briefcase and prepared to finish the job.
Gorse knelt by the body and again blocked the airways
to satisfy himself that he'd behaved professionally and
the man would feel nothing. After all, he wasn't a
monster.

Using Gun Hill Station carried a benefit beyond
ground level tracks. He was concealed on the trackside
just beyond the end of the northbound passenger
platform beneath the train station. His initial intention
was to throw the body onto the tracks after the train
began rolling slowly forward from the station. The body
could not be present on the tracks before the train left
the platform because the driver would see it in the
headlights. He wondered whether the trainman would
feel the popping of bones beneath steel wheels. Then he

had discovered a notice on the station door that express trains would not stop at Gun Hill during the current renovation. He confirmed the notice on the IRT web site. So when he saw lights of an approaching subway, he lifted his victim and rolled him forward as the train clacked past the platform at speed. The body missed the front wheels and landed on the track a moment before the rear wheels of the front car and all the wheels thereafter shredded it like a food processor. Gorse turned to grab the briefcase and tossed it beneath the wheels of following cars.

When the taillights of the five train vanished to the north Gorse crossed over the tracks and climbed the ravine, discarding the bolt cutter into a thicket. As he drove to the airport, he wondered what the news would say. Did the dead guy doze and overshoot his station. Did he try to exit while the train was moving? Did he fall walking between cars? Suicide? Gorse had read incidents were common enough that ambulance chasing law firms specialized in signing up families of riders killed or injured on the subways.

Gorse's face was unremarkable save for his nose, pressed in like a boxer's. It had been broken and an eye socket fractured in a long-ago beat-down at the direction of an FDC guard during his stay at South Florida Reception Center. The name of the place sounded like a welcoming pull-off along the interstate with fresh-squeezed orange juice and maps to Kennedy launches and the Magic Kingdom. It did not suggest a state penitentiary in Miami-Dade drawing male felons from jails across nine counties. Youthful Gorse was made a guest of the juvenile justice system, but the prison's population was a crowded cross-section of inmates of myriad ages and offenses. It's where he'd been befriended by Griff Cameron.

Deep lines descended from the outer edges of Gore's lips in a perpetual frown as a consequence of a lifetime barren of joy. His hair was ibis white and cut toothbrush short. The hair on his forearms was silver and wiry. He wore heavy glasses with frames of black plastic, and when he smiled, which was seldom, others could be excused for misreading it as a sneer.

He thought about the dense grove of trees on the hillside. It had triggered a memory. He knew what it was called. A copse. He had looked it up long ago when it appeared in a poem by Wordsworth. A poem about nature being integral to life and love and human character. He felt that way about Florida Bay and the Glades. It was a long poem but his favorite verse was a single line. "Nature never did betray the heart that loved her." He had been drawn to books of English poetry in the prison library and read them all more than once. Poetry fed a hunger in him. After all, he wasn't a monster.

Chapter 14

The hour was late and Vento Fagan elected to take a cab home from LaGuardia. It beat the tedium of the bus and subway link and chopped the travel time by more than half. He opened the door to his apartment, expecting the customary frenzy of welcome from his unflaggingly enthusiastic bulldog Zippy. After the Zipster was satisfied he had administered the proper amount of drool upon his much-missed master the dog remained by the door and whimpered softly. Vento grabbed the leash and was irked that Zip had been forced to endure marking time in distress. Where was Emmet? He should have been home hours ago. Walking Zip was part of the deal. He could only guess Emmet met someone at Maguire's and had lingered downtown. He'd chew him out in the morning. When Zip was restored to guileless amiability and withdrew to savor a bacon biscuit, Fagan stowed his small suitcase in a closet and poured two fat fingers of single malt Laphroaig. Just the one and to bed. Must be at the train platform in seven hours.

The message from police had come during the night and was left on office voicemail with a return number to call. "…to notify you that a male victim carrying documents suggesting he was an employee of Grissom, Bennett and Heyward was found dead on IRC tracks on the Dyre Avenue Line last night." A personnel manager had followed up first thing in the morning. No identification was found on the body. May have been taken in a crime of opportunity. There were some homeless camped nearby. But several documents spilled from a mangled briefcase bore the name Emmet Vance. Word spread through the office and was met by wholesale shock. No one was more shocked than Vento Fagan, who had been assigned to train the new recruit two weeks earlier. Emmet was a rising star of Security Systems Administration, and had been poached from Wells Fargo. Fagan was tasked with bringing him up to speed on the company's IT architecture and nearby watering holes. Emmet's hotel stipend was elapsing and his lease on an apartment wouldn't begin till the first of the month. Fagan made a proposal to their mutual advantage. Vento was heading to Boston for a weekend seminar on systems integration which happily coincided with a Labor Day weekend three-game Yankees-Red Sox series at Fenway. Vance would move out of his hotel and into Fagan's apartment to dog-sit and would fly solo for two days behind the desk in Vento's office. As internal cyber-security, he didn't deal with the public. If the rare call came from the switchboard, just say Fagan and take a message. No sweat. The holiday meant Emmet could enjoy a few days in the greenery of the neighborhood outside the urban crush of FiDi before returning to work Tuesday, and Fagan would return the following night for the changing of the guard. One question answered. Vento had ridden the morning train alone because Emmet was dead. Dozens of questions remained. A Channel Four news push on his phone queried whether Vance was drunk on the train. Would the post mortem find drugs or alcohol as contributory to the accident? Vento had seen no sign of impairment following drinks after work, when he had introduced his protégé to his go-to pub on the way to the train. Granted, Emmet hadn't been an associate long enough to reveal bad habits, but he had not arrived at GB&H on the same track that Vento had: criminality. He was Ivy League, for fuck's sake. Not an epicenter of reckless choices. Vento's ordered mind began putting two and two together. His thoughts during the commute had been concerned with something else entirely. He had made it clear before he left for Boston that he expected Griff Cameron to share the details of their partnership without delay, and Griff had given his assurance that he'd lay out the road to riches as soon as he took care of something. He promised to reconnect within forty-eight hours. Fagan had put the matter out of his mind in Boston. But checking messages this morning, there were none from Griff and it had been six days since their last exchange. He knew Griff well enough to suspect deceit. He'd been snowed. Previous conduct should have tipped him that Griff had no intention of cutting Vento in on his colossal hustle; whatever it was that would back up the money truck for unloading. And Griff knew Vento well enough to know he would leverage what he knew to cut himself in on the payday. He'd still be in the dark about the Morgan Stanley account without Fagan's intercession. So why had Cameron not sent a follow-up email? Because he knew there was no need? Because he knew that Vento Fagan was dead. Griff seldom dirtied his hands so there was a stooge. When one delegates mistakes can happen. Emmet had been working at Vento's desk and living in Vento's home and walking Vento's dog. It didn't take a Harry Bosch to surmise that the killer saw the performance of Emmet Vance in the role of Vento Fagan and didn't have the Playbill to inform he was watching the understudy.

Eventually Griff would realize Vento was still breathing, but not, perhaps, till after the bearer shares were discovered. Fagan dialed his boss.

"Hey Stan. This Emmet thing hits me hard."

"I know. Everybody's thrown for a loop. Crazy."

"I'm feeling kind of overwhelmed, you know?" Vento lied. "We were real friends, you know? I saw the notice that the company is bringing in a counselor, but I think I need some time to get myself together. Away from the office. Everything here is a reminder."

"Totally get that, Vento," said Stan. "Take some time. Deal with it. Call HR and tell them I okay three days bereavement. More than that comes out of your vacation days. We'll need you back on your game when we pick an alternate. Didn't know you guys were so close. Accept my sympathy."

Fagan hung up and leaned back in his chair, watching through the glass wall of his office as staffers milled around jawing about the day's drama. He stiffened, rolled forward, pulled up a browser and entered *American Airlines*. The reservations page remembered he had used La Guardia and LGA magically appeared in a text entry box labeled *FROM*:. Into the *TO*: box, Vento entered the letters *MIA*.

Cal awoke early and headed north. He enjoyed exploring university libraries an easy drive from the top of the Keys. From the Schooner Wharf Bar the distance to Florida International University and the University of Miami were identical. He knew the business school at U of M had a nifty research library. But it was a virtual library with subdued designer lighting and stylish computer work stations. Cal preferred the smell of books. FIU's Green Library had books and was open twenty-four hours. He'd need a computer, but would savor that old book smell. He prowled the stacks and pulled histories tracing the growth of the companies and biographies of their founders.

He strode from the elevator into research services and asked for authorization to use a station in electronic resources. He took a seat beside a young man hunched over a screen, ears tucked inside headphones, fingers flashing over a keyboard nestled in his lap as cartoon fighters battled with fists and death rays across a landscape of mountains and pagodas.

Cal pulled up the Mergent Archives database. Mergent had acquired Moody's long ago, and Moody's was the chronicler of American business in the long ago. In search criteria he metaphorically set the flux capacitor to 1929. He looked up Ford and checked the progression of capital stock history. Then Firestone. It had been bought by Bridgestone. He made a note of that outcome respecting the shares. Edison was swallowed up by McGraw. McGraw bought out by Cooper Industries. He recorded the prices paid for those shares. He moved on to Hathaway. Okay. Oh, here's what that became. Cal scribbled notes, calculated total shares after splits and logged the ups and downs of the securities over the nine decades the bearer shares had waited patiently, somewhere. At last, he exited the database and Googled a stock quote site. He retrieved the current share price for Ford. Then he typed in the name of the company that Hathaway morphed into, and he blinked when he saw the current price per share. It took a couple of beats of his heart to register. "Holy fucking shit," murmured Cal, a man famous among his friends for being congenitally unable to swear.

Chapter 15

Milo hung up after being told to buzz off by Morgan
Stanley in Manhattan. He'd decided one can always ask,
and he asked for information about the Edison
marketing account balance. The answer was predictable.
"In compliance with federal law our client data is
confidential unless you have a court order stemming
from a legal criminal investigation or are one of the big
three credit bureaus." In other words, take a long walk
on a short pier.

The first follow-up to Milo's scattershot emails
dispatched over the holiday was to the Edison birthplace
in Milan, Ohio, a bucolic canal town whose glory days
of commerce were extinguished by the rise of the rails
before the Civil War. Harvey, the man who answered
the phone, expressed regret that Milo had not been
present for the Milan Melon Festival, the highlight of
Labor Day thereabouts. Yes, the museum displayed
some vintage phonographs. No, there was nothing out of
the ordinary among the few cylinders in the collection. It
was an investigatory dead-end, but Milo scribbled notes
to put by for an oddly random sidebar story. It happened

the museum possessed the only Grammy ever awarded to Thomas Edison: the 2010 technical award lauding him for inventing records and movies and electric light. But there was a striking irony in the award which tickled Harvey, who had plainly told the story a thousand times.

"See. When the Recording Arts Academy cooked up awards in the '50s, it batted around names for the trophy. They wanted it to be memorable like the Oscar. Somebody said how about the Eddie, for Edison? He invented recording arts and sciences, for Christ's sake. But when they saw sketches they decided the tabletop Gramophone, the British version of Edison's archrival Victor Talking Machines, was more elegant, with its classy horn and flat record, than the Edison cylinder machine. They picked the Gramophone and the Grammy's were born. So Edison received his gold-plated award for technical achievement in the form of a player that helped drive him out of the record business. Ha! How 'bout them apples?"

In his next call Milo didn't have to pull teeth to extract information from the archivist at the Edison National Historical Park in West Orange. Mason Frost was chatty in the extreme. He was cheerfully brimming with enthusiasm at the opportunity to gab with someone interested in tapping his vast reserves of all things Edison. Calling up a profile picture, Milo saw an affable man in his late thirties or forties. Broad of face and smile. His voice a mellow baritone. His manner urbane. Frost described himself as a lifelong Edisoniac. He had grown up a mile from the museum and first visited on a school trip. After that he would ride his bike to the laboratory complex and poke around whenever his

allowance would permit. He earned a Communications
Masters in-state at Rutgers and wrote his thesis on
"Edison the Business Failure," analyzing the many
financial risks Edison took to produce new technology
and consumer products that went nowhere and the
pragmatism that gave him confidence to dissolve
corporations and lay off many workers as he shifted
from one business venture to another. Frost described
how Edison formed and discarded dozens of companies.
He took flyers and risked capital in scores of worthwhile
industries. But it often came to pass that others had more
aptitude for operating in those industries than Edison.
Like home construction. Edison got into the business of
building houses of cement put up with a single pour into
a mold. He even made cement record player cabinets.
"Neither were hits with the public."

Mason traced his career path from Museum
Technician to Park Guide to Public Affairs Specialist to
a Curator GS 11 pay grade with the National Park
Service. At last an opening appeared at the West Orange
factories and his mastery of the Edison chronology was
swiftly recognized. When one of the original Edison
manufacturing buildings was converted into residential
lofts, he rushed to get a mortgage. He could walk to
work in four minutes. He was saving to buy a Tesla.

Milo found that curious. "Didn't they hate each
other?"

"Too strong a word. They had a fundamentally
different view of electrical physics and whether an
inventor's first loyalty was to the science or to the
business. Tesla's was to the science. You remember the
quotation that is more or less accurate, where Edison is

asked if he's frustrated not getting results perfecting his storage battery. And Edison's reply is always something to the effect that on the contrary, he's gotten tons of results because he has learned several thousand things that won't work. But Tesla considered Edison's habit of throwing everything at the wall to see what sticks completely unscientific. Both guys threw shade at one another after their association had ended. Snark is nothing new. Tesla had a pretty good put-down of his more famous ex-boss. He said, 'If Edison had a needle to find in a haystack, he would proceed at once with the diligence of a bee to examine straw after straw until he found the object of the search.' Tesla's point being that application of a little theory and calculation would have saved him ninety per cent of his time and effort."

Milo knew the feeling. He'd been reaching in the dark this way and that in the search for the phonograph needle in a haystack. Like Edison, he'd been throwing everything at the wall and little had stuck.

Mason said, "But I calculate this is all off subject."

Milo decided he'd spent enough time establishing empathy with Frost. It was time to get to the point. "My rule is to assume it's all useful. But as I said in my note I'd like you to direct your focus to what you know about the promotional and advertising side of the company. There is a school of thought that there was some sort of contest in 1929 that was cooked up to promote sales of Edison records. But when I used the Rutgers Edison papers search engine and called up meeting minutes and memos from 1929 no mention of that contest popped up. There were references to other contests."

"An Edison Records promo stunt in '29 doesn't ring a bell." Mason paused to think. "Let me do a quick preamble and then get to the narrow focus part. Edison was one of the master promoters of his time. Edison's genius wasn't just as a guy who created all sorts of brand new technology consumers didn't even know they needed. Edison pretty much invented the cult of celebrity. He cultivated the legend of his own genius and became the living logo of all his products. If today everybody in the world who hears KFC can picture the image of the Colonel, in his day the whole world knew the image of Edison because it was plastered on every item produced by the four thousand workers who used to punch the time clocks here. He was prone to seasickness and hated the transatlantic crossing. But he traveled to Europe anyway not only to learn about emerging technologies but to give the power elite of Europe the opportunity of worshipping at the altar of Edison. Edison lunched with Gustave Eiffel in his private penthouse apartment in the Eiffel Tower and gave him a phonograph. It was a great photo-op. His ad men were forever coming up with gimmicks and inventive ways to keep a buzz going about whatever Edison was selling." Mason paused and switched gears. "Now having said that, it would be odd that Edison would invest big in a campaign for phonographs or records in that year."

"Because of the stock market crash?"

"No. Because Edison Records was floundering. Charles Edison was in charge by then. And after considering arguments for and against committing resources into regaining lost market dominance, he very suddenly decided to pull the plug in October right before the market tanked. Just a few months earlier Edison loudly touted its new disc records which were made to be compatible with record players of other brands. The Edison recording studios were still operational that summer. And audio experts agree that the Edison players and records produced the best sound. But the truth was that Edison had never made a profit on disc records in the seventeen years since the firm jumped into that market. The department heads debated the pros and cons of sticking with records right into the first week in October. There was internal griping about sky-high money demands by the top pop artists.

Everybody in the company knew the old man loved the record division like the prized racehorse in his stable. But his horse had come up lame and the decision was made to put it down. The order to dump the whole shebang came the week before Black Thursday and the decree from the front office was draconian. The order went out to make it all go away by the end of the year. By December thirty-first, in just ten weeks, Charles Edison wanted all recording stopped. All contracts with artists were cancelled and all inventories of records liquidated. Some master moulds of recordings would be shipped off to the Henry Ford Museum or sold. No returns by sellers would be allowed. All cylinder records in stock at the factory would be burned. All employees would be cashiered. The record factory would be retooled to make radios and on the first of November its new name would be the Radio Division."

Milo considered that. "The cylinder I mentioned in my email. With Edison's voice. Could it have been burned with the other cylinders?"

"I can't be certain but it's doubtful. Recordings of the voices of famous people were saved for their historical importance. Can't imagine anybody would knowingly destroy any cylinder of Edison's own voice. But again, I never heard of this contest. And I would remember hearing Edison's voice promoting it."

"You've written books about Edison, right? If you haven't seen one iota of info on this contest, maybe I'm on a wild goose chase."

"Well. Not necessarily. Going all the way back to when Edison was in his prime, he was a fierce guardian of his own public persona. He never threw anything away. He preserved his Menlo Park early records and built a vault to protect them. In 1928, he created a historical research department here at West Orange to organize the tons of records his businesses produced. The historical department also acted as the public answerman to inquiries from the press and scholars. We hold around five million pages of documents and only about ten percent has been microfilmed or digitized for public view. Somebody once calculated that if all the documents were placed end to end it would take more than twelve hours to drive past them at seventy miles an hour. The Rutgers digital online collection has maybe a hundred eighty thousand records that are searchable by metadata. New stuff is added all the time but the online database will never include everything. Researchers still come here to look at the actual paper. There is so much of it storage has always been a challenge. Rutgers has been archiving the records since the Seventies and is still at it. There are still materials from the last couple of decades before Edison died in 1931 that are in their original file boxes, but most have been organized by subject matter. From the start the material was categorized in terms of historical importance, and those tagged as of less consequence got pushed to the back to get around to someday. I could find time tomorrow to rummage through some of the more obscure documents now that you've given me the year and department. I'm always looking for an excuse to visit the archives."

Milo had continued to record and send to the station daily reports offering conjectures about possible motives in the museum murder. But Barry groused about a lack of progress and without a breakthrough Milo sensed he was running out of leads. Things were taking too long to fall into place. A call to the University of California Santa Barbara produced no breakthrough.

He was connected to a cylinder historian named John. The UCSB archive streams digitized recordings of Edison cylinder records online. No, John had never heard of a recording of Edison's voice promoting a contest hyping the phonograph division. "And I would have heard it. We have more than ten thousand cylinders and I've heard 'em all. Speeches by famous people who have been dead a hundred years. Pop music by songwriters who have been decomposing way longer than they composed. Vaudeville routines and arias and military bands and fiddlers. We curate two terabytes of digitized Edison records. Very big in Blue Amberols and Edison early wax. You'll ask how a needle can ride in a wax groove without shaving it smooth…" Milo, in fact, would not ask that question, and when John began to hold forth on the chemistry of fatty acids and metal ions, he broke in with another.

"Everyone I talk to says the Edison phonographs had the best sound. So why did the competition win?" John was easily steered.

"Because Edison had banal, oldfangled taste in music. And remember he was deaf as a croquet peg. He would make decisions about instrument placement by biting a phonograph with his teeth to feel the tonal vibrations. Victor and Columbia and the rest produced records way more appealing to the modern masses than Edison's stable of artists serving up a stale mix of Stephen Foster, military bands and cornpone comics. And he refused to pay to get the top singers and musicians other companies like Columbia were making into superstars. Edison liked sappy and schmaltzy. His favorite song was *I'll Take You Home Again, Kathleen*. The public wanted jazz. Edison hated jazz."

It appeared Milo had touched a nerve mentioning sound quality as John's tone grew more emphatic and he turned to a spirited defense of old stylus analog recording compared to modern digital. Maybe relevant was he doing a feature piece for NPR, but zero help in getting his ball through the uprights. Milo interrupted to end the chat but John was on a roll and talked over him.

"And think about that golden record they sent into outer space. On Voyager? That was an analog record. It'll take Voyager forty thousand years to get to the

closest planetary system. And aliens there will have to
build a player that turns at 16 and 2/3rds RPM to hear it.
But the record was made from copper coated with gold
and should last a million years. Chuck Berry is on there.
Johnny B. Goode. Mariachis made the cut, too. Most of
it is classical, to impress the neighbors. But then there's
Blind Willie Johnson and his bottleneck slide guitar
singing into a Model 394 Western Electric condenser
microphone for three minutes and twenty-one seconds in
1927. It was a Columbia record. *Dark Was the Night,
Cold Was the Ground* was mainly humming and
moaning. But spacefarers who hear it won't have to
understand language to get a sense of what it is to be a
human Earthling. That record could someday be the only
music still surviving after the planet is a cinder."

This appeared to conclude John's Ted Talk and with
relief Milo said thanks and disconnected.

Milo updated his notes and imagined a blessed day
when the name Edison no longer intruded into his day
planner. His corkboard cards formed two lines: What he
knew and what he didn't. The first line was a short one.
He hoped somewhere among the pile of Edison minutiae
he'd collected was a key to making headway. But the
well was running dry and time was running out. Milo
had always been good at puzzling things out. But a
puzzle can't be finished with pieces missing.

His phone announced a text from Cal. He'd found
something useful and was on his way back down the
Keys. Beyond that he was reluctant to provide details
over the phone. He'd assemble the brain trust at the
Wharf tomorrow.

That suited him. Enough for today, thought Milo. He recorded a fresh report suggesting progress in his investigation and forecasting an imminent major breakthrough. He hoped it was the truth. He opened the fridge, popped the top on a Victoria and settled into the couch. "Alexa," he said. "Play Coltrane." Milo loved jazz.

Chapter 16

Saturday, September 28, 1929.

Dougal Brogan was sheltered comfortably enough in a railroad crew quarters on Long Key. He could be collected by the northbound passenger train out of Key West later in the day if the weather improved and if track damage was not great. It was the 28th of September. He had hitched a ride late Friday on a small worker transport train dead-heading north in the night. But halfway up the Keys came the signal to halt. The secondman descended from the crew cab to open the trackside call-box and ring up the dispatcher. The hurricane forecast had been relayed to the railroad and the warning encompassed the entire Keys. Rising winds placed empty freight cars at risk of tipping. As reports from ships placed the storm center barreling toward the Upper Keys after causing widespread ruin in the Bahamas it became clear that the trains would be secured in the more sheltered depots until it passed in the morning. The new directive was for the engineer and crew to advance a short distance to tiny Craig Key on which there was a siding where they would ride out the storm inside the locomotive.

A person from whose uniform he took to be a conductor came to share with Dougal the change in plans. On his copper badge was engraved the name Douglas. It occurred to Dougal to wonder if it was a first or last name. Douglas reported the worst of the blow would likely hit above Key Largo on the mainland miles ahead. He allowed as how a steam engine in a hurricane was no place for an Edison man and suggested he overnight in an FEC work camp on Long Key out of harm's way well south and west of the storm's eye. The wood-frame shack had a wood-burning iron radiator with a cooktop and the trainmen assured him the storm would pass in the afternoon during daylight. They may even return to retrieve him before dark, conditions permitting.

Brogan had completed his assignment for the Old Man early the previous morning. He enlisted the help of a train yardman at track's-end who commandeered a terminal maintenance car to shuttle him to the chosen place. It wasn't far. Working together the hardware had been installed and the materials hidden within. Back in Key West the worker gave him the key and went on with his busy day. The yardman's memory of his unusual task would swiftly vanish in the rush of work to complete before the storm arrived. Dougal's northbound itinerary included information-gathering visits over several weeks to multiple Edison sales offices along the Eastern Seaboard. To send a dispatch to HQ he had walked to the big red building that was the Key West

Post Office and dutifully jotted a note (in the impeccably
fluid handwriting his pious wife warned would lead him
to the sin of pride), relating an account of his day's
mission accomplished. He asked that duplicate keys be
acquired from the manufacturer to insert in record
packaging containing clues. He was intentionally cryptic
in his choice of words to avoid disclosing too much in
the event the parcel was misdirected or intercepted.
Then he directed a postal clerk to enclose the letter and
the key in a sturdy envelope crafted from thick fibers of
unbleached Philippine hemp, addressed to the home
office. During mid-day, the winds increased and he
reluctantly concluded, against his better judgment and
suppressing his anxiety, that an Edison executive's time
was money and he could not delay his rail travel.

He was spooked and afraid of hurricanes, because the
damage done across Miami and up to West Palm Beach
just three years before had knocked trains off tracks and
snapped telegraph poles in half. He remembered reading
where the storm surge smashed into the Hollywood
Beach Hotel and afterward survivors found dunes of
sand drifted halfway to the ceiling in second floor
rooms. It was that 1926 storm that caused the University
of Miami to name its football team the Hurricanes and
its mascot the Ibis—the first bird to flee before a
hurricane and the first to return after.

And just last year another monster storm breached
the dike at Lake Okeechobee and drowned two thousand
five hundred unfortunate souls. And that was on the
mainland. By now everybody knew the surges could be
far higher in the shallow waters of the Keys.

But the trainmen assured him that on the Florida Bay side of Long Key he would be sheltered from the full force of the wind and the level of surge the railroad weather office forecast to arrive above Key Largo. He debarked from the Long Key depot near a fish camp made famous by writer Zane Grey. Would Zane Grey stay here if it was dangerous? He made his stumbling way over a short track spur and from the oaken crossties his nostrils filled with the scent of coal tar. He found an assortment of small rustic cabins constructed of pine with floors fixed atop posts intended to keep feet dry in the event of some unusual tidal or storm event. As the time passed ploddingly at a leaden tempo he would describe as adagio, or perhaps largo, his curiosity emboldened him and he opened the door on the shielded bay side of the cottage. Morning's first light dimly penetrated leaden clouds. Close by was a fence and beyond stretched a broad sandy promontory overlaid with patches of coontie and prickly pear. This coarse landscape gave way to clusters of seagrass past which one's range of vision could only just make out a rocky beach. Despite his cautious nature he found himself mesmerized by the roiling sea and sheets of wind-whipped rain and airborne fronds propelled out of sight over the ash-grey horizon.

As he braced against the wailing wind and witnessed the bending palms and churning waves in rapt wonder, he became aware of a rising sound, a low bass added to the higher pitch of the keening tempest. A doleful howl he would describe as lugubrious. As an Edison adman he liked to be precise in language, a trait his wife called excessively persnickety. The sound grew louder, more a vibration than a noise, and he could not even hazard a conjecture as to its source or direction of origin. He could not know that the barometer had dropped perilously with its lowest reading of 954 millibars recorded by railroad instruments at Long Key. He could not know the storm had already caused historic damage in the Bahamas. He could not know that as it approached its ferocious buzz-saw headwinds were pushing the sea ahead west and south up the rising slope of the seabed and driving the building waves one atop another into a natural curvature in the coastline that concentrated and accelerated the flood tide as the Atlantic collided with Long Key. He could not know that the official feet-above-sea-level at Long Key was zero. He could not know that the sea on the ocean side of the narrow island had now heaved up a rushing bore four feet above the height of the island, racing to join the waters in the Bay. He did not know this until the crushing water wall appeared to his right and to his left around both sides of the shack and joined together in an unremitting embrace, lifting him up on its monstrous shoulders across the field and beyond the beach into the sea. Close behind him followed the splintered wreckage of the obliterated shack. He had never learned to swim but knowing would have been of no consequence. He did not drown. His panic and his life ended concomitantly as a snapped tree trunk driven longways smashed his skull like a pile-driver.

Word of what had happened to Dougal Brogan reached the West Orange offices in a terse telegram from the Florida East Coast Railroad. The rail crew had survived harrowing hours in which the sea had

overwashed Craig Key but with insufficient force to
move the train. Debris blocked the tracks and two
crewmen set out on foot the following day to retrieve
their passenger, to find that the company camp had
disappeared entirely. In the absence of his body,
Dougal's name was not even appended to the official
death toll. The missing man's colleagues pinned up
newspaper accounts of the catastrophe. They read that a
nine foot surge smashed across a portion of Key Largo
where one gust was measured at 150 miles per hour.
They read where surging tide drove waves entirely
across the narrow middle Keys and that sections of the
still-under construction overseas highway were washed
out as far down as Big Pine Key. That train service to
Key West was blocked by damaged rails for a week.
And that days passed before the Coast Guard stepped in
to start resuming mail service in and out of the island.
That is why the delayed arrival of the parcel from Key
West at the Edison offices in mid-October was cause for
unease and gloom among the missing man's colleagues.
Few had knowledge of Dougal's task in Key West and
none but Dougal knew its every detail.

When the envelope appeared the Edison family and
staffers were consumed with preparations for the Jubilee
to take place the following week. Henry Ford was
dedicating his Americana museums in Dearborn where
Edison's Menlo lab had been reassembled, and Edison
was the main attraction. He was to illuminate a bulb in a
re-enactment, to the precise minute, of his historic
achievement fifty years before. Americans were to
douse their own house lights for the evening and switch
them on at the same moment, although the execution of

this instruction was on the honor system and would
doubtless ignored by most, who were using electricity
anyway to hear the event on radio; broadcast on one
hundred forty stations. President and Mrs. Hoover were
to gather at the lab with A-list celebs like Madame Curie
and Will Rogers and Orville Wright. Albert Einstein
would offer greetings on a radio hookup. The current
objective in West Orange was the arranging of
connections to the steam train that would deliver the
boss to the Smiths Creek Station platform which Henry
Ford had acquired for his Edison homage because of its
back-story. Edison's carefully burnished biography had
it that a conductor kicked young Tom off his train onto
this platform when the boy's chemicals ignited a fire in
a baggage car. Sometimes the telling of the yarn would
be embellished with the damage to the boy's hearing
having been caused by the trainman's rough handling.
But to Ford, even as mythology it made the depot
platform museum-worthy.

To all but a handful of insiders at the West Orange
home office, the enigmatic delivery of the cryptic note
and the single key was a bewildering mystery. An omen,
perhaps. A dark warning from the victim of one disaster
of disaster yet to come. This interpretation was, to some,
born out three days after the Jubilee when Wall Street
began the collapse that would erase the wealth of a
nation.

The decision to shed the money-draining record
division had been made even before the crash. Schooled
by his father in the art of extracting TAE, Inc. from
failing enterprises, Charles wrote off his losses and
forged ahead resolutely, closing the books on Edison

Records and reassigning managers who survived the purge to other departments. When Mort Hall reminded him of the hidden contest prize, Charles appraised with melancholy the shattered stock market and declared that expending manpower to locate and recover the devalued and noncommercial certificates would be a squandering of corporate resources. Came the order—Abandon it all and turn the page. In the rapid-fire dissolution of the division, no one thought to pass the order to The House of Morgan.

Chapter 17

Vento Fagan watched the woman walk from the parking lot till she disappeared within Griffin's office door. He took the chance that he had enough time. He walked to her car and clicked his frequency scanner to unlock the driver door. From his pocket he withdrew a thumb-length plastic box. Ducking below the steering wheel he found the diagnostics port and plugged in the small dongle. He locked and closed the door and returned to his rental. The woman's car was now linked to his phone. The software self-installed and already showed the car parked on a map on his screen. If undiscovered it would record and save location data for all trips for the next thirty days. It would not take that long.

Fagan watched the man emerge from Griffin's office door. It was the first time he had seen the man but he knew him in an instant. The man was fireplug stocky and muscular. His nose was flat like a journeyman boxer's. Central casting for the role of goon number one. He'd bet money this was the killer who had not murdered Vento. It was time to introduce himself. He followed the man as his car turned onto the street. When the man parked at a bar at a mile distant, Fagan pulled into a slot nearby. He waited till the man was inside. In less than three minutes the man's car also acquired a tracking device.

Entering the nearly empty bar, he claimed a vacant stool beside the man who believed he was dead. The man was sipping from a glass tumbler containing amber liquor on ice. Fagan turned his head to face the man. "You have me at a disadvantage. You know my name, but I don't know yours." Gorse did not react. He returned his empty glass to the bar with apparent disinterest. To satisfy himself he hadn't followed the wrong man, Vento leaned close and spoke again softly. "My name is Vento Fagan," said Vento Fagan. Now Gorse showed interest. He processed the words, and turned to look at the stranger. He remembered the name. It was an unusual name. He remembered the mangled corpse on the track.

The bartender appeared and Vento pointed to Gorse's glass and extended two fingers to include himself. He turned back to Gorse. "Mistaken identity is a funny thing. Always tracks back to a fumble. Somebody dropped the ball. Do you remember when Sydney Carton traded places with Charles Darnay and was carted off to the guillotine to save the life of the husband of the woman he loved?" Fagan had also filled many lonely hours at the prison library. "I was always skeptical about how that impersonation was pulled off. Okay, like me and Emmet Vance the two dudes looked like each other. I get that. But one was an Englishman and the other was a Frenchman. Had the jailor or the

executioner spoken to the prisoner for just a moment
they would have known he was the wrong guy. But then
I put myself in the place of the jailer and the
executioner. Caring about it was above their pay grade.
They did the job. They were cogs that drove the wheels
of the Reign of Terror. Like you. Deliver the man.
Separate him from his head. Nothing personal." Fagan
shook his head slowly and mournfully.

"But we both know Griffin Cameron. You know him
better. Know his intolerance for failure. Murdering the
wrong man is unlikely to be received with a shrug.
Rather it is likely to result in termination." He leaned
into Gorse and repeated softly, "Termination."

Gorse recognized truth and knew his error was
compounded by the off-script murder at the museum.
Cameron had miraculously conjured a benefit from that
slip-up which conferred upon Gorse a lucky pardon. But
two such mistakes were unpardonable. He was fucked.

"But I'm not Griff Cameron," said Fagan. "Yours
was a fatal error but not to me. It saved my life and I am
disposed to imagine we can throw in together for a
common benefit. Cameron believes me dead and that
frees me to take from him what he means to take from
me. You are thinking you could kill me now. But you
blew your advantage." Fagan patted the outline through
his shirt of the pistol in his waistband. "I am now the
hunter and I can take care of myself. And consider this.
Griff ordered me erased to avoid a split that would have
still made him stinking rich. Once you deliver the stocks
he will have to make a call about the only man alive that
can link him to murder. I'm thinking it unlikely you will

report this meeting to Griff. You are not Sydney Carton. You won't place your own head on the chopping block."

Gorse was unaccustomed to independent thought but recognized he had no play. He was a practical man. Having an option is better than having none. After a while he turned to Fagan and spoke. "I'm called Gorse. You ask questions. I'll maybe answer them."

The barman delivered four more drinks before the two men left the bar separately.

At his Coral Gables office Cameron offered additional ideas about how Danny should reconnect with Milo. Invite him for lunch? Better to meet at her hotel pool. She should wear a swimsuit. He was too engrossed in the new stuff coming in to sense her revulsion at the implication. His thoughts were elsewhere. Griff was now receiving the reporter's emails. Gorse's mission inside Milo's home had been two-fold. Leave the paper clue. And to worm his way into Milo's email client. The insertion of the keylogger program was misdirection. Any competent inspection of the computer would turn up the malware. Cameron's real objective was to hijack the email settings. That had been made simple when Gorse identified Gmail as the webmail provider. Griff instructed Gorse to enter settings and open the forwarding option. In the input field Gorse entered the address of an account controlled by Cameron on a cloud server in Belize. Gorse checked the box instructing Gmail to leave the original message in the inbox as new and unread. The forwarding option was a normal function of Gmail and because the setting was

presumably chosen by the user it would raise no red flag
unless the change was discovered by Milo. How often
does anyone check email settings? Replies to Milo's
queries provided Griff with a window into his thoughts.
The Edison factories guy seemed promising. He would
be looking where no one else could.

Griff switched gears and pulled up a list of
webmasters Danny would phone to pitch translation
services. He'd return after lunch to follow up. At half
past ten she completed her calls and typed up her report.
Griff would be pleased. Three potential clients agreed to
meet. Her misgivings about deceiving Milo did not
infect her office work and she cold-called with
enthusiasm. She assumed Cameron's business product
was a useful and marketable tool. She saved her report
and clicked print. A message appeared. Printer ink low.

Danny opened a desk drawer where she'd found
cartridges. Nothing. She checked a closet and found
paper but no ink. Vexed, she continued searching the
office. The space had once been an apartment living
room and a bright and airy bay window framed a
cushioned seat. The bench seat was hinged and she lifted
it to reveal a storage compartment. She opened and
closed a box containing a rat's nest of computer cables.
Behind the box was a bag of dark gray. She lifted what
revealed itself to be a backpack of heavy canvas. She
placed it atop the box and pulled open the zipper. The
interior was dark and she reached in to feel for a
cartridge box. Her hand touched an object and her tactile
memory matched it with an object she knew. She lifted
the object from the bag and held it in her hand. A
cylinder record. She placed it on the floor and spilled out

the rest of the bag's contents. Dozens of cylinders. Some enclosed in cardboard capsules and some unboxed, like the first. She tried to dismiss a piercing stab of apprehension by imagining explanations. Griff had worked where there were an abundance of cylinder records and he was, in fact, hunting for one in particular. But she knew as she examined one after another what she was seeing. The titles of these recordings matched the list Milo showed her in Fort Myers. The list of records stolen from the Key West museum. By a killer. Danny had grown up tomboyish and not easily frightened. But she now felt a creeping coldness as she tried to push from her mind the thought of what would happen if Griff walked through the door at this moment.

Danny gathered up the cylinders and returned them to the backpack. All but three. These she stashed into her handbag. She closed the window seat after restoring the contents as best she could to their initial appearance. Her thoughts were a jumble. Police? Self preservation overrode the instinct to involve the authorities. She works for the man she now believed for a fact to be responsible for murder. She'd be tarred with the same criminal brush. It was probably Mr. Gorse who'd done it but her cousin directed everything Gorse did. She and Gorse never spoke beyond the casual greeting on the rare occasions they passed at the office. She had wondered what Mr. Gorse did for the company. He certainly seemed the opposite of a computer type. That he would be capable of lethal violence was suddenly no surprise. If Cameron knew what she'd found, she sensed with a horrible conviction that in the face of a threat her cousin would not dither over spilling the blood of a blood relative.

Her mind flashed on her two days in the company of Milo Bird. In their time together he struck her as empathetic. Not a jerk. He radiated sweetness in company with pheromones. He seemed suited for the role of an advocate. He might know what to do. He might even believe that she hadn't known. She hoped so. Of course, revealing what she'd discovered to Milo would make him a threat to Griff, too, but she reasoned that Griff already saw him as dispensable. She should warn him at the very least. Danny returned to the desk and typed a line beneath her report, explaining that she was unable to print. She asked that Griff let her know where to find cartridges and that she would call tomorrow. She left the document open on the desktop. She locked the office and walked to her car. Danny sat quietly for a while. She sent a short text to Milo. She started the engine.

Milo awoke late and scanned the newspaper and again found no mention of the museum murder. The reporting staff had turned its attention to other things. They probably checked in daily with detectives, who were reticent to share more than the standard press platitude; as ritualized as a congregational call and response. "Any progress?" "The investigation is ongoing." Milo was reasonably confident any breakthrough had eluded the print press absent of photos or fingerprints. Not that he was closer to the killer than they were. And did he want to be closer to a killer? He was much closer to calling the whole thing off. He was usually dogged, but now was just weary. He had some time before he joined the others for lunch. It was ordinarily a Green Parrot day, but it was agreed that they could be more easily overheard at the Parrot and they trusted Wharf bartenders to be discreet. He was sweeping leaves from the porch when a tone alerted him to Danny's text. She needed to share something important. She was driving down and should arrive in Key West after two. Will he be home? Milo texted back—she could join him and some friends at The Wharf. He typed simple directions to what town fathers two decades before had renamed the Historic Seaport, ballyhooed as more appealing a destination to tourists than Key West Bight. He wondered what was up. What thread of sham would be loaded into her web shooter to weave her net of fiction today? No matter, he thought. His reporty-sense assured him uncovering secrets worked both ways. On his phone he pulled up the weather. Maxine had been upgraded to a Cat 2 overnight and had brushed Haiti's north coast with punishing winds reaching to Port-au-Prince. Its center had, some hours before, ravaged Matthew Town, the only community on the little-populated Bahamian Inagua Islands, midway between Turks and Caicos and Cuba's east end. Some talking heads were comparing the projected track to Donna, the Cat Four killer that wrecked the Keys on the 10th of September two weeks before the first Nixon-Kennedy debate. Others compared its route to malevolent Georges and Irma. One weather wonk recalled it following the path of a cyclone that sank a Spanish treasure flotilla in 1502 while

Christopher Columbus rode out the storm on the leeward side of Hispaniola. The experts still bet on high level winds to temper her ferocity. Far-flung outer bands were to deliver local rains in the afternoon and landfall was forecast after sunrise tomorrow.

With time to kill he leaned back on his porch and read a few chapters of the new C. J. Box Joe Pickett novel. Trails of snowmobiles and moose through high timberland of back-country Wyoming was a far cry from Milo's flat, hot, watery, crowded habitat. Then he locked his door and ambled his way to the docks.

Chapter 18

The gang chewed over some bar bites and rumors before ceding the floor to Milo. He described the contest that wasn't. He explained that the motive for murder was money, astonishing no one. The money would come from cashing in the grand prize: some old stock certificates. "Cal went up to FIU to look up the stock history and total up what they'd be worth today. It would be best if he explained it. It'll take some telling." Cal's pals were always in for a penny and a pound. His disquisitions were invariably enlightening and even entertaining. Milo took a sip from a smooth Reposado and chased it with Pacifico. His expression was unreadable as he repositioned his stool to face Cal five heads away.

Cal spread photocopies of printouts over the bar. He sipped the foam from his beer and waited till all had been likewise topped off. "First off," he began, "the reason the contest went bust is a no-brainer. They pulled the plug on selling records. But it was a one-two punch. Then came Black Thursday and Black Monday and

Black Tuesday. As a second punch it was a doozy. The Dow dropped like a Carolina-rigged heavy sinker baited with a jumbo leech. By the end of November the market was down forty percent and the worst was still to come." Cal slipped handwritten notes from his shirt pocket.

"Actually, Edison marketing in hindsight probably thanked their lucky stars it killed the contest before the crash. Can you imagine trying to interest anybody in a contest in which the first prize is a bunch of stocks? What's second prize? A Valentine's Day trip to a garage wall in Chicago?"

"But let's just get to the stocks. I guesstimate the value of the stocks when they were socked away was somewhere around twenty thousand; each company's contribution worth roughly five grand. But that's a meaningless number. I began by finding out how many times the stock has split since 1929. When a stock splits the owners who hold certificates don't have to surrender them. The transfer agent managing the account simply adds the new shares to the total. Stocks go up and down but all these years later what matters is today's price per share times the number of shares. Naturally, most of the stocks have had dividends accruing to them which presumably have been residing in an interest-bearing account for four generations and that'll be a nice bonus. Also, sometimes dividends were paid in stock. So we may have more shares than we think. Any questions?"

The day's onstage troubadour capped off a spirited rendering of the Piña Colada Song with a flamenco flourish to a smattering of applause from tourists at the far end of the bar.

Cal pressed on. "Let's start with Edison. The National Phonograph Company was reorganized and renamed Thomas A. Edison, Inc. in 1911. Most of the performers in the Edison corporate circus were under that big-top. Son Charles took over in '27 setting dad free to putter around the lab in the Florida sun. Charles ran the company for thirty years and served as Acting Secretary of the Navy for FDR in the '30s. He became Governor of New Jersey but his dad must have been spinning in his grave like a waxy cylinder because Charles ran as a Democrat. In the late '50s the company merged with McGraw Electric to become McGraw-Edison, and Charles became chairman of the board. In the '80s stockholders were bought out by Cooper Industries, which paid sixty-five dollars a share. We started with a hundred shares of Edison. In 1946, the stock split 30 to 1. So our hundred shares became three thousand. After the McGraw merger it split two for one, and split again in 1965. Now we have twelve thousand shares. So in 1985 here comes Cooper Industries paying us sixty-five dollars for each of them. It's a buyout so our brokerage account managers cash out and Cooper marches onward without us. Our payday is seven hundred eighty thousand dollars, not counting accumulated dividends. We are happy." Each member of Cal's audience took a moment to weigh the magnitude of their imaginary wealth. They did appear happy.

"Firestone is next. In 1906, Henry Ford chose Firestone tires as original equipment on all Fords. Harvey Firestone made a profit of five dollars a tire. Twenty bucks a car. By 1913, seven years later, Firestone grossed fifteen million dollars selling tires at a time when an entire Ford car cost five hundred bucks. That would be three hundred eighty million today. Firestone stock got pumped up like the rest in 1929 then took a hit but it stayed profitable through the Depression. It bounced back and puttered along for many years at around ten bucks a share. In 1971 it split two for one. Then came the biggest thing ever to bump up Firestone stocks."

"Firestone was selling for thirty-five dollars in 1988 when Bridgestone paid eighty a share in a bidding war against Pirelli. It was the Japanese against the Italians in a battle to become a major player in the American market. It was a buyout so we get eighty bucks times the number of shares. I stopped everything when I found out about Hathaway so I don't have a complete history of Firestone splits, but if we start with a hundred shares in 1929 and just factor in the 1971 split that makes for two hundred times the eighty dollar buyout. We have at the very least, sixteen thousand dollars without adding dividends."

Some of Cal's listeners frowned in disappointment. They'd hoped for more. Compared to the hundreds of thousands in Edison shares Firestone stocks amounted to no more than pocket change. Ford Fiesta-level money at best.

"Of the four companies, only the Ford name remained unaltered as a corporate entity into the new millennium." Millie Mae silently refilled glasses as needed. This was not Cal's first soliloquy. "Ford's golden age dimmed as the calendar clicked off the lights on the 20th Century. In the financial collapse of 2008 when taxpayers bailed out the big three car companies

Ford became a penny stock. Even so, Ford stock split a number of times into 2000. I have to cross-check other references, but it looks like a hundred shares of Ford in 1929 divided like an amoeba into twenty thousand shares as of the mid-nineties. A hundred and fifty-five thousand at today's prices, plus dividends and interest. Now I have to note that in 1929, nobody but the Ford family and Ford Foundation owned shares of Ford Motor Company. Henry said Ford would be taken public over his dead body. Which is what Henry the second did, actually. So Ford himself gave Edison the only shares of stock not family-owned for his contest. Edison, Inc. was also closely-held, but it is likely both men intended to buy back their shares presuming that the contest winner would prefer cash."

"Now we come to the Hathaway shares. In the mid to late 1800s, New Bedford, Massachusetts was arguably the richest city on the planet. It's where the whaling ships brought home the oil that lit the lamps of the civilized world. Herman Melville sailed out of there. And the super-rich seagoing families added spinning mills to their portfolios. Horatio Hathaway was one of the filthiest of the rich. He was heir to the money bin of the Buzzard Bay Hathaways. His dad and uncles left him a couple of the biggest cotton mills and he sat on the boards of directors of other companies running seventy factories providing work to more than forty thousand laborers; mostly immigrants and some as young as eight or nine. Anyway they started converting mills from water and steam power to electric motors even before the light bulb. But the move from gaslight to electric sped up the change and Edison experts

consulted with Hathaway on choosing the right
generators and dynamos and wiring. Horatio later sat on
the board of directors of New Bedford Gas and Edison
Light. Six years after Edison first lit lower Manhattan,
when New Bedford was bright with Edison lighting,
Horatio expressed his gratitude for Edison's help in
adding to his own prosperity with a gift; a chunk of his
own personal shares in his new textile company,
Hathaway Manufacturing. Giving stock to Edison was a
wily ploy of more than one tycoon to provide a pretext
to boast of their close connection with the great man."

"As a thrifty business decision it's likely Edison
elected to re-gift his Hathaway stock to his treasure hunt
to reduce the number of shares contributed by him and
his friends. Anyway, back in June of 1929 Hathaway
Manufacturing stock sold for forty-nine dollars per
share. So the Edison marketers took an even hundred to
make its portion of the prize just under five thousand."

"So we have a hundred shares of Hathaway. Those
certificates have been doing nothing since 1929. But
that's not true of the company. Hathaway split four for
one in 1948. So we have four hundred shares. Hathaway
merged with another textile firm in 1955. Berkshire Fine
Spinning Associates added its first name to Hathaway.
In the merger we get four shares of the new company for
every share we owned in Hathaway. So that gives us
sixteen hundred shares. Now comes Warren Buffett."

"Is he Jimmy's dad?" asked Millie Mae.

Cal smiled. "No, but a reasonable question. They
both got asked that so many times they took a DNA test
to see if they are related. It turns out no. But Jimmy is
worth more than a half a billion and is a Berkshire

Hathaway stockholder and he goes to the shareholders meetings. When he and Warren meet they call each other cousin. Anyway, Warren Buffett bought Berkshire Hathaway in the early sixties and it expanded over time to be a corporate umbrella over a vast collection of properties. It's the third biggest public company in the world. You probably know the name but you are likely unaware how you contribute to its profits."

Cal read from his notes.

"When you buy a Dilly Bar at Dairy Queen. You buy it from Berkshire Hathaway. When you paint your hallway Desert Rose with Benjamin Moore you pay Berkshire Hathaway. When you buy your fiancé an engagement ring at Helzberg Diamonds. If you are line-dancing in your Tony Lama Boots. Hathaway makes money when you shave with a five-blade Gillette. When you buy a double-A Duracell to power that Gillette. You can buy a house through a Berkshire Hathaway realtor. Berkshire Hathaway owns a hundred percent of Fruit of the Loom and GEICO Insurance and smaller chunks of Bank of America and General Motors and Coca Cola and a legion of logos of corporate America. Flying somewhere? It's the biggest stockholder in Delta and United and in the top three at American and Southwest."

Cal raised his eyes and posed a question. "You watch Channel 10 TV in Miami?"

Milo said, "Who doesn't? Julie the weather girl?"

"You know she was once a 49ers cheerleader," said Mack.

Diego said, "I don't know a guy who would disagree that Julie is flat-out number one in keeping you distracted during a hurricane."

Cal said, "It happens that Channel 10 is 100% owned by Berkshire Hathaway."

"So we own part of Berkshire Hathaway. And guess what the closing price of one single share of Berkshire Hathaway stock was yesterday on the New York Stock Exchange?" Cal paused for effect.

"Four hundred thirty thousand dollars."

"Four hundred thirty thousand for one share?"

"Correct."

"And how many shares are in the prize package?"

"Sixteen hundred."

The Eskimo clasped his rough meaty hands behind his head and leaned back with eyes closed, apparently working on the calculation in his head. Cal saved him the effort.

"At yesterday's closing price that's six hundred eighty-eight million dollars. Who knows how much we add to that in dividends and interest?"

"Christ on a cracker." Ben said. "That's Powerball money!"

The Eskimo asked, to no one in particular, "What would you do with all that cash?"

Mack had been doing some calculations. "Well for damn sure I wouldn't hire no investment advisor. Hell, my interest checking pays point-two percent. On upwards of half a billion that's in the very nice neighborhood of more than a million a year without touching the principal. And I would be all about committing serious assault and battery on the principal. Just dump it all in checking and spend the rest of eternity visiting the ATMs of the world!"

Don Diego said, "Milo, would you keep the stocks if you found them?"

Milo shrugged. "Hadn't thought about it. I've been thinking about the contest prize in the abstract. Not a real possibility. And it still isn't. I have no idea where to look for it."

As everyone processed the new developments, Junie looked at her phone and handed it to the Eskimo. Some time ago she had demonstrated that when she was expecting a delivery she could call up a screen map that showed the location of the truck as it moved. For the Eskimo, it was discovering a new form of entertainment. He studied the maps intently and tried to predict the most favorable route the driver must take to negotiate his cartoon truck through the Key West street maze, factoring in one-way streets, as it stopped to stock bars and eateries before arriving at Schooner Wharf. He and Mack would sometimes pass the phone back and forth, not infrequently engaging in a heated disputation with the course-plotting algorithm over which route would be most efficacious. He placed the phone on the bar and Mack leaned in. The game was afoot.

Milo's phone vibrated. A text. Mason Frost. It was a brief note. He read it twice. Then he said, his voice rising with excitement, "Listen up. This is from the media guy where Edison worked in New Jersey. He was checking something for me and he just sent this." He read aloud from his phone. "Hi, Milo. I spent some time in the archives after you narrowed the parameters of what you were looking for. Rooted around in uncurated boxes of documents from Edison Records advertising meetings in the last year of the department. Sorry to report that there was no cylinder recording of Thomas Edison reading the directions to a contest prize." Milo looked up with a grin into downcast faces. "Here's the last line. Mason writes, 'But how would you like a copy of the script he read from?'"

Chapter 19

The most recent rain band had passed. Milo stepped to the boardwalk to phone Mason Frost.

"You know you sort of buried the lede, Mason. You…are a national treasure."

"Well, thanks. Wasn't all that much. This morning I found some time to follow your lead. I went to the stash of documents ranked non-essential archived in boxes and folders from the year 1929. These hadn't yet been microfilmed or curated digitally. And from 1929 I singled out memos and meeting notes that were generated by the marketing and advertising staff only. I'd been at it less than twenty minutes when I came across a file folder containing minutes of a meeting discussing details of your contest that was later called off. In that file there was also a brown paper envelope. In the envelope was the script."

"Damn!" said Milo, admiringly. "You gotta come on down to Key West, Mason. Your money's no good. We'll do an epic pub crawl!"

"I may take you up on that when the nor'easters blow. I'm curious to find out how this turns out. By the way. There's something else. Also in that brown envelope was a key."

Milo was doubly stunned. "I don't suppose you can send me that key?"

"Ha! Not a chance. Everything here is the property of the National Park Service and the revered taxpayers of these United States of America. I can take a picture of it for you. I'll send you that with the scan of the document."

"That'll have to do, then." Milo had a thought. "Just one more favor. In addition to a photo of the key would you scan both sides of it? Scans will give me the exact size and shape of the key, in case there's something I can do with that. Maybe have one made."

Mason promised to send an email with images within the hour. Milo returned to the group and reported.

"So, this is getting ahead of ourselves, but before actually reading the script laying out the clues, it would seem Mason may have put his hands on the roadmap we can use to put our hands on the stock certificates."

Don Diego said, "But only if you can verify they are still worth the paper they're printed on after ninety years."

"That's what Ben's been doing. Hey Ben, you're up."

Ben Cobb was tall and thin. His remaining hair of grey appeared as shrinking islands behind his ears, nearly submerged in a rising sea of alopecia. He took a pen from his pocket and reached for a printout of lunch specials. On the bar he flipped it over and scribbled, and handed what he'd written to the bartender. "Please write this on the board big enough for everyone to see." Millie Mae took the paper wordlessly and stepped to the blackboard. With a well-used cloth she erased the soup and sandwich special to make room. Taking yellow chalk she copied the word Ben had written: ESCHEATMENT.

"Let's begin with the interesting origin story of the excellent word escheatment." Ben snuffed out the rump of his Partagas Robusto in a large Cinzano ash tray. "Long ago and far away in the days of Kingly England and the knights of yore, the king owned everything and private ownership was a favor bestowed by the crown. When a landholder died without heir, the crown took the land back, or assigned it back to the overlord who had parceled it out, because it was in escheat, which means "failure of heirs." It was common law and common sense, because otherwise the land would lie fallow to the benefit of no one. But after the American Revolution the Founders fiddled a bit with English common law. Taking the Fifth usually means not having to testify against oneself. But the Fifth Amendment also says the government may not take private property for public use without just compensation. That means when a state takes unclaimed property and converts it to money to use in its general fund, it is acting as a custodian of the property for the original owner, and must repay that owner at any time he or she shows up to make a claim. Some take that to mean that if a state sells unclaimed stocks the owner who turns up ten years later would get paid the price of the stocks as it was at the time they were sold. Others say that's not fair and the owner should get the value of the stocks as they are when the claim is made, assuming that would score the claimant more money. But now forget about all that. Because escheatment does not apply to these unclaimed stocks and here's why."

"If I were in court I would argue that, in the case of the contest stocks, the shares are in limbo between issuer and owner. The transfer was legally begun but not consummated. The stock cannot be escheated to the state as custodian of unclaimed funds because there was never an owner to claim them. The process of the state acquiring a dormant intangible property like shares of securities can only begin after strict due diligence is conducted to endeavor to contact the owner, usually by certified letter at his last known address. Stock certificates are tangible; you can touch them and hold them in your hand, but they are just symbolic, representing the share in ownership of a company, which is not something one can touch or hold. These particular stocks are fashioned as temporary bearer shares owned by whomsoever is in possession of them. They are, in effect, owned by no one, until they are. The countdown to escheatment will not begin until the owner is identified. Ownership of the shares does not occur until they are discovered. The account restrictions on the transferring of the shares impose no expiration date and the stocks in the contest brokerage account are not considered transferred until a winner takes possession, at which point the clock begins ticking on potential escheatment by the state."

"The state where the owner lives is first in line to acquire unclaimed property and currently our imaginary owner lives nowhere. Since there is no owner of record for these shares, they are not subject to escheatment because the state has no right to escheat property from

someone who does not own it for the purpose of giving
it to someone to whom it does not belong: The State.
The axiom of escheatment is that the state may take
custody of property owed to another person who has
failed to claim that property. But in the case of the
missing shares, the person to whom the value of those
shares is owed is a phantom, not yet flesh. Therefore the
property is unclaimed only because it has no owner and
ownership cannot then be transferred from no one."

A few of his listeners lifted their glasses to Ben, who
took a bow and sat.

He said, "So we work on the premise the clues will
lead to the stocks and the stocks are worth a fuck-ton of
money."

There was a tap on Milo's shoulder. "Hi," said
Danny.

She had stopped at home only long enough to pack a
small bag and was still wearing the casual white pants
and black blouse she wore at the office. Her sleeveless
top displayed slender arms of light caramel and her
open-buttoned neckline revealed sun-tinged skin taut
over collarbones curving to meet olive shoulders.

The men at the bar sat up straighter and with effort
shifted their gazes from the newcomer to Milo raising
ten inquiring eyebrows.

Milo said, "This is the reporter I told you about. The
reporter who's not a reporter."

Danny's first reaction was to feel deflated at having
been found out. As an undercover agent she'd given
herself a passing performance review. To have not been
convincing at all was a blow to her ego and she was
inclined to be indignant. But she knew that was stupid.

This complicated things. She'd rehearsed her penitent confession in her drive across the Keys. And she'd expected Milo would be surprised and sympathetic as she prostrated herself in sackcloth and ashes. But if he'd never believed her from the start, why would he believe her now?

"I came to tell you everything I know." Danny spoke softly. "Can we talk somewhere?"

Milo chinned toward the others. "This is my fact-finding commission. Multiple heads are better than one and such. They are my think-tank when I'm stuck. I'm stuck now and they are on the case. Tell your story to them and if you convince them you're on the level we'll be good."

Danny looked at the five nameless men seated at the bar and the two women behind it. They didn't comprise a proper jury but they were certainly a bar association. She pushed aside embarrassment and searched for words to win their trust. "My name is Danny Carreras. I was working for the Miami Latino paper but I quit to work for my cousin. The money was better and I'm trying hard to get out from under. I work in his office and one day he asked if I would help him find out something important. He told me about the man's murder at the museum and he swore on his mother he had no connection to it. He said a man he met in prison who now works for some financial company in New York was the killer. He told me after the murder this man who did it called him to ask him to help find a cylinder recording that could make them both rich. He knew my cousin was working at the Edison museum and figured he might be in a position to help. My cousin's name is

Griff Cameron and it's no secret in the family he's been into shady things. But he told me he would never partner with a killer and that he turned him down. But he decided to find this money for himself. I believed him. That he didn't have a part in the murder. He said he would pay me a big bonus if I could find out where the money is. When I say big I mean three hundred thousand dollars. He said a reporter was investigating the museum murder and he might uncover some leads that could point me to the money. So I agreed to meet the reporter and find out what he knew. And that is all of it. All I knew about it. Until today."

She recounted the events of the morning and her discovery of the stolen recordings. She retrieved the three from her purse and the cylinders were passed down the bar. The jurors, interested, examined the evidence. She told them she now was certain beyond doubt that Griff wouldn't think twice about killing again and told them about Gorse, the minion she believed was the assassin. She looked at Milo. "He will come for me. When he finds out where I've gone. He will come for you."

Her listeners felt her fear and adjudged it genuine. Milo turned to them. One by one they nodded, and Millie Mae and then Junie smiled and raised their thumbs. Milo took her hand and shook it. "Now that you've defected from team Griff, welcome to team Milo."

Cal said, "Accessory after the fact."

"Say again?" said Milo.

"She provided assistance to a killer for a time after a murder in full knowledge the motive behind the

homicide was missing stock shares. Shares she
continued to search for. And aware that her cousin, who
enlisted her in the hunt, had committed crimes and
served time in prison. We are all compassionate
empathetic people, inclined to overlook certain
imperfections of character to which we all secretly
admit. But we should presume the state attorney won't
be."

Milo said, "Something to consider. And there's
something else. If we call Jack Matthews he will round
up Griff and this other guy and Danny and the stolen
cylinders will seal the deal and that's that. Call the next
case. Even if Danny testifies against her cousin she's
still labeled an accomplice and since Griff is a snake his
defense is he says/she says and he deflects whatever
criminality he can onto Danny. She's a collaborator and
fair game for indictment. The State doesn't care about
Edison's defunct promotion or long lost stock
certificates. Somebody killed Nathan Parker in a
criminal conspiracy and they caught the conspirators.
On the other hand, if Danny helps find and recover the
shares, and we hand them over as prosecution's
evidence as to motive, Danny's rectitude is
rehabilitated."

Mack said, "Not to mention you get to dive into a bin
of money like Scrooge McDuck."

Milo grinned, "If the court in its wisdom eventually
declares finders keepers."

Danny frowned, "But now that you all know this, if
you keep quiet about it you're in trouble, too. And if you
keep it from police, they can't know they need to protect

you from Griff. I wanted your advice and help in getting me out of this mess, not to pull you all into it."

Milo looked down the bar. "I will state unequivocally that absolutely no one present overheard anything you said as you were confiding your suspicions to a journalist working on a story."

Ben said, "But circling back to what she said. When you say he will come for us, is that along the lines of a general sneaking suspicion or might there be a hard timetable for that?"

"He doesn't know I'm here. I don't think he does. He won't know I've gone till I don't show up for work tomorrow. When he misses me, he and Mr. Gorse will come. He can't help but suspect I'm disloyal. Especially if he finds I've been into the stolen cylinders."

"So this Mr. Gorse," said the Eskimo. "It figures he's the guy who knocked Milo around. So he's been in the house. You can't stay there. Neither of you." The others expressed agreement. "So I think you best come stay on the boat with me."

Milo saw the wisdom in that. "And we don't know to a certainty he's not roaming around town looking for her now. So we'll head to the boat and I'll fill you in when I try to decipher the clues."

"Better still," said Cal, "We all decamp there together and speed things up a bit."

They drank up and settled up. As Milo promised to relate developments to Junie, she leaned over the bar and kidded with a sly smile, "So how old is she?"

Danny felt grateful for the protective support from Milo's friends, but felt some unease about what sort of primitive sleeping arrangement she'd encounter on what

she imagined was the rustic fishing vessel they called
"The Polly" where lived the Eskimo. Until she saw the
boat.

Chapter 20

The Eskimo wasn't an Eskimo, although he answered to the name without resentment. He didn't like to be called Inuit, a member of which people, anthropologically, he certainly was. He renounced the title of Inuk, the singular of Inuit. Rather, he identified as a Nunavummiuq, an ex-pat of the vast territory of Nunavut, three times the size of Texas in the most distant limit of Canada's north on the far side of yonder. His name at birth was Moses Ashoona.

Moses learned to fish commercially in the footsteps of his stern *ataata* and his kindly *ataa* before him off the coast of the Beaufort Sea. It is often said the Inuktitut language contains many words to describe ice, and the Eskimo often said that as a boy he aspired to live where ice was less integral to one's vocabulary. One day he stuck out his thumb and hitched a ride in the opposite direction of the Arctic Ocean and traveled south till he ran out of it. He signed on with fishing boats, with crab boats, with shrimp boats. He apprenticed as a boatyard hull cleaning diver. He learned to dismantle and rebuild diesel engines. He calmed the tantrums of pumps and generators. His face was wide and flat; his body compact and thickset. He was possessed of steely forearms and rock-hard triceps that had pinned many a challenger's knuckles to bar tables. Not yet forty, he was a crackerjack seadog. And he was content to have found a home where the chief vocation of ice was to keep fish fresh and drinks cold.

Moses was currently in the employ of a Grand Rapids snowbird who had won the multi-state lottery. With his windfall he bought a McMansion on Mackinac Island where he resided in the period between blizzards and a large boat he docked in the Historic Seaport in Key West as a winter refuge from the frozen northland until the arrival of hurricane season. It was a 100-foot luxury yacht of Italian manufacture. Each of five staterooms had bathrooms and there were crew quarters for four, if he ever required a crew. In point of fact the Lucky Polly had never left Key West Bight since its delivery from a Miami yacht broker. The owner used it as a floating hotel for his family and guests. Marina rules banned guests without the owner present and nixed liveaboard caretakers, but lottery money bought expensive amendments to the liveaboard contract.

His stewardship of the Lucky Polly was quiet and efficient and the Eskimo and the dockmaster were on good terms. Inside the garage compartment within the stern resided two PWCs, inflatable trampoline, kayaks, snorkeling equipment, paddle boards and other amusements. The use of these inside the marina was prohibited so a small tender was garaged for excursions beyond the breakwaters. The Eskimo kept the engine and mechanicals in trim and shipshape, but the yacht would likely remain stationary until a new owner was piped aboard.

Milo's posse knew the yacht's salon well, having taken comfortable shelter there when the occasional blustery cold front drove them from the bar. Seating could easily accommodate twenty and they numbered seven. The rule was to leave it as they found it and communally chipped in to replace withdrawals from the fridge and liquor cabinet. Mack distributed beers and Danny filled a glass from a premixed bottle of margaritas. A computer resided on a desk in a corner. Milo called up his email and printed the attached documents. He produced and distributed copies to everyone. Then he read the email text aloud. "Mason writes, 'So the minutes of the meeting lay out the long and the short of it. Ten treasure hunt records would be distributed randomly around the country. Each would contain your train ticket voucher for necessary rail connections and another store voucher to claim your free phonograph. Also, a key and two one-hundred-dollar bills; enough money in those days to pay expenses of those following the clues. All music cylinders are inscribed at one end with the title and performer and catalogue number of a song. These substituted cylinders and the labels on the flat records were to be inscribed instead with the words, "To the train, carry the ticket. To the hiding place, carry the key." So you come home from the store and open your record and you find the stuff and a congratulations certificate explaining the contest. Then you play the record and hear Edison reciting the clues. I suppose you'd have to write them all down to carry with you. It never got that far and there's no mention of printed clues.'"

Milo turned back from the screen and said, "Now here is what I've thought all along so maybe this could make things simpler. We know that some company guy involved in setting up the contest was talking with the Florida East Coast Railroad about the best place to hide some package. And we have all these Key West Edison connections. Look at the photo of the key Mason sent. The initials FEC are stamped right on it. Now nobody reading the clues from Bumfuck to the back of beyond would know any of this, so they start from zero. But I think the package was hidden somewhere along the FEC railway and I wouldn't be surprised if it's close by. Edison premised his contest on *Treasure Island*. He lived near the Gulf and a day's sail from the Dry Tortugas. At the start of the book pirate Billy Bones tells drunken stories of the wild deeds in the Tortugas before he drops dead and young Jim finds the map in his sea chest. If I'm a contestant from Ohio or Vermont or the Dakotas riding the FEC looking for treasure, I'd want to ride right down here to where the Gulf breeze rustles through the palms. So think on that."

All eyes were on the papers in their hands. In his head Milo tried to hear the words in Edison's voice as he read aloud.

"Strike off to meet first sun illuming Maine to Spanish Main
Then descend to dexter pendant on 27's chain
From the Spanish Main a crook'd bony finger points the way
Where pirates hounded tall ships filled with riches

at the quay
Riches great remain there still to make your life a
pleasure
Near where remains Maine's slain remains awaits
unburied treasure
At terminus of travel ends one pathway to your prize
Afoot, turn whence you came and espy your path
materialize
Your hunting hounds' names are Holes and Keys
Together they lead over land and over seas
Follow their tracks to the East from the West
They shall guide you at last to the end of your quest
One Key of many, its name is the treasure,
X marks a hole, on a green path of leisure.
South of lake's center, between two and three,
to the track is your track,
50 paces straight measure.
Heaped stones are the border; steel a footstep too
far.
Turn that way and this way, to fix your lodestar.
Fortune hinges on hearing. It calls to you clearly.
Mr. Edison congratulates you most sincerely."

"Cool," said Mack.

"Starting point is East Coast for sure," said Ben. "Everybody go east to the coast to start." There was unanimous agreement.

Don Diego asked, "What's dexter?"

"That one I know," said Milo. "I'm left-handed. My mom teased that made me sinister. Lefties are sinister. Righties are dexter. Turn right at the coast and descend."

Danny had only today descended down the chain. "The chain is the Keys. The pendant hanging from the chain is Key West."

"Florida is the 27th state," said Cal, because he liked others to know that he knew things.

Mack said, "The next lines are just confirming that. Florida was part of the Spanish Main and bony fingers are again the Keys pointing to Key West."

"And dead sailors from the Battleship Maine are buried in Key West," said Don Diego in the stentorian tone of voice with which he told that story daily to his riders.

There followed a period of silence as they read ahead and thought it out. Milo spoke, "Like I said everybody's traveling at this point on the FEC and the terminus has to be the terminal at the end of the line. The station where everybody got off the train. On Trumbo Island."

From his Conch Train narrative Don Diego recited, "Trumbo Island was named for Flagler's railway engineer who built the island out of landfill." He added, "You can see it through the window right over there. The Navy and Marines share it."

Mack said, "Hope it's not there. It's restricted."

"It's not there," said Danny. "The next line says when you get to the end of the first path you turn around and take a second path."

"Now what?" asked the Eskimo. "Holes and Keys? A keyhole?"

"Maybe it means more than one thing," offered Cal. "We have a key to open a lock. But the keys are a recurring theme. And the line that comes next speaks of being led over land and over seas. The Keys are the land. And the track from the mainland to here was always called the Overseas Railroad."

Milo nodded approvingly. "So we're off the train but back on the tracks. On foot. Going back the way we came."

"One Key of many, its name is the treasure."

Again silence. The only sound in the salon was Mack pouring himself another beer. Mack repeated, "Its name is the treasure."

Milo and Danny got there together. They burst out in unison, "Stock Island!"

There was a lively ovation as each of the others in turn spoke the words aloud. Stock Island. "The golf course!" said Mack. "The green path of leisure. A hole on the green path. I played it a week ago. The Key West Golf Club."

Don Diego again put on his tour guide hat. "Built by Langford and Moreau Golf Architects of Chicago. Designed as an 18-hole course but only nine holes were built before it opened in 1924. Dynamite was used to blast away coral to lay down fairways. During the 60's nine more holes were added. The layout was redesigned in 1983 by Rees Jones to accommodate the inclusion of homes with golf course views. Still the only golf course in Key West and the southernmost golf course in the continental United States."

"Whoa, there's a fly in the ointment," said Cal. "Two redesigns since these verses were written. South of lake's center, between two and three. Could be these directions don't apply to the golf course today."

Milo returned to the computer and called up the club web site. No words were spoken as he worked. A wind-driven sheet of rain drummed on the salon windows. After ten minutes he turned and smiled. "The site displays the original 1924 blueprint design. And that design has been reworked quite a bit. But comparing the original map with the scorecard map for the current Rees Jones design it is pretty apparent holes two and three remain in their 1924 locations with significant changes. The direction of play has been reversed. Hole four used to be west of hole three. Now it's east. And the lake has been moved from the front end of two in the old design to the front end of two going the opposite direction. Comparing the two maps, the original 1924 lake between two and three—would be located today on the green approach on the second fairway just above the tee on three. That's where X marks the spot. Close enough for government work. Come on over and check out the satellite view on Google maps." With the crowd gathered around him, Milo pointed out the location of the old lake on the map. "This is where we begin the next clue, but you can see that the exact spot doesn't matter so much because of where we are going next. Fifty paces straight to the FEC tracks. The tracks were ripped out eons ago but the Overseas Railroad turned into the Overseas Highway and Route 1 is the old railroad right of way. We just walk from here straight to the road and turn this way and that way and see if there is still something to see. That would put us on the north side of the road somewhere between Cross Street and MacDonald Avenue. Can't see any structure in this photo that would need a key. Still possible whatever it was is long gone."

"Let's go!" exclaimed Mack. The ex-Special Forces instructor was always ready to advance on an objective.

Milo observed, "It'll be dark soon. And we don't have a key. We have photos of the key. Let me try to find out about that. Besides, a gang of seven people poking aimlessly around in the dark along the only highway into town in a downpour will attract bothersome attention and cops. Let me work and we'll head over tomorrow. Hurricane hunkering will keep traffic light. But just Danny and me. Low profile. Guy and a girl in hoodies in the rain, just trying to make our way home." There were grumbles of disappointment.

"You need me with you," insisted Mack. "Don't forget there may be bad actors hunting you. I'll bring my sidearm." Milo didn't argue the point. "Let's make it early. Get here at six."

After some excited rehashing of the day's work, the group gradually disbanded, leaving Milo, Danny and the Eskimo to consider the next move.

"I want to try something," Danny said. "When I was working a university excavation and someone would uncover some unfamiliar object that was a mystery, I would take a picture. Then I put it into a search on Google images. That compares the photo to thousands of others and displays all the similar images. Do it with the key. See what comes up."

Milo nodded. "That's a good thought. But first, there's a guy I know who might have some insight off the top of his head. Hope he's reachable. Usually knocks off at five." Milo keyed a contact on his phone. Just when Milo was certain he'd be detoured to voicemail purgatory the line was picked up. A voice sounded annoyed.

"Rails Museum. We're currently closed and will stay closed Friday because of hurricane conditions. Open again ten AM Saturday. Thanks for your interest."

"Al! It's Milo. Glad to find you in. Why there so late?"

"Watching paint dry. For real. Touched up paint and have fans on it so it's not tacky when we open up again. What's up? You at the Wharf?"

"No. I need to run something by you. Can I shoot you a photo by email?"

"Sure. I need a diversion. Did I mention I'm watching paint dry?"

Milo pressed send. Al Stein was a friend of many years who could be counted on as an expert voice on light features about the history of sailing and the railroad in the evolution of Key West.

"Got it," said Al. "Was hoping for more of a challenge. Too easy. Adlake number forty-eight steel switch lock. 1912 patent. Key is hard cast bronze. The forty-eight was a workhorse railroad padlock for more than a generation. The railroads loved them because the steel locks were cheaper and worthless to scrap metal thieves who targeted the brass locks that came before. Adlake short for Adams and Westlake of Chicago, New York and Philadelphia. They moved to Elkhart in 1927 and are still in business. Still making locks for the transportation industry. Dozens and dozens of railroads used it to lock up switches to prevent some Snidely Whiplash scoundrel from pulling the switch and sending a train down the wrong tracks."

"Great. So here's my situation. Say, theoretically, you needed to unlock one of these padlocks to open something, and you didn't have a key. Could you get one?"

"Oh goodness me, yes. They made tens of thousands of these lock sets and they are so simple in design and sturdy in construction a lot of them are still in use after more than a hundred years. Maybe not so much for locking up switches but for padlocking sheds and storage areas and trackside call boxes and such. You can do a search for Adlake forty-eight switch lock and find them for sale on eBay and railroad collector's sites. The trick is matching the key with the railroad. Each railroad had its own signature lock configuration with the keys manufactured with the bit on the end customized with slots to fit the particular lock of each railroad. So your FEC key would only fit an FEC lock."

"Do you know a collector I could call right away? I don't have time for eBay."

"No. You can just come over here right now. I got a bucket of 'em."

Milo had been stunned so many times in a single day he was almost numb to this latest miracle.

Al continued, "Yeah. Here's the thing. Back in the day trainmen were issued a standard key which fit all the locks of the same type down the line. Losing a key was a serious offense. When conductors traipsed off to the local saloon they left their keys in the custody of their wives. But keys get lost. So the manufacturer would sell replacement keys in lots of four dozen. Lots of railroads didn't need all those so they got put away and sometimes when the road went defunct they'd wind up in railroad museum gift shops. That was my idea when I found a bucket of ancient FEC keys at a yard sale. Figured they'd be good to sell as souvenirs in the gift shop. But Joe Doakes from Anytown don't give a shit about some old key to a lock that ain't there just 'cause it has FEC stamped on it. Shit, he don't even know what FEC is short for. And he's on his way to the next bar anyhow and he's overdue. So come on by. Take a handful for all I care."

Milo explained to Danny and Moses where he was going and said he would swing by his house and move his car nearer the marina for tomorrow's run. Danny felt a bit crestfallen. She had looked forward to some alone time with Milo without his entourage. The terror she felt when she arrived had evolved to exhilaration after the day's events, and when she looked at Milo she felt awakening arousal. She felt the tingle of desire. Her body suggested to her that what would be very nice right now was a good…and then Milo said "Good night" and the Eskimo said, "I'll show you to your stateroom." She lay in her bed studying the cabin ceiling, waiting. When she did not hear Milo return, her last thought before surrendering to sleep was "What a senseless waste of a yacht and tequila."

Chapter 21

Gorse picked up. "Saddle up, Morris. The game is on. I need you in Key West. Now."

Gorse checked the time and calculated he'd arrive after dark. But he could find the reporter's house blindfolded. He assumed that was his assignment.

"Bird has his hands on what he needs to find the stocks. I've been studying what he got. An email from some museum guy. The directions are given as a puzzle but it seems to end up at a golf course. And it involves the old train that used to run to Key West. On a map the only golf course I can see near there is the Key West Golf Club. It's on Stock Island. Cute, huh?"

Gorse didn't get it. "So I grab Bird?"

"If we had time I could find it. But I have to assume he's on the scent now. There is another part to it that requires a key and without the key he may be stalled. There is a picture of a key. Maybe he gets one made. But what if he can get into the hiding place without a key? We need him to take us to it. And by that I mean persuade him. In that special way you do."

"I'll be there before nine. I can douse the lights to his place from outside."

"Listen carefully, Morris. If he's not home. I need you to keep him from reaching the golf course until I arrive. I'll throw some stuff in the car and book rooms for us in town. Should be an hour behind you. Do you have it with you?" Gorse knew he meant a gun. "I have it."

"I'll bring one, too," said Cameron. "There's more. I called Danny. Wanted her to connect with Bird. Find out what he's doing. She didn't pick up. Got voicemail twice. I bought her the phone for client calls so I can track it. The track went dark in Islamorada. She must have turned it off heading down. She's already in Key West. If she's cut off contact I suspect she's out for herself. Figures Bird will find it and there's no payday for second place."

"So I find her, too?"

"You do that. And Morris. This is important. If there's no sign of them, go to the Key West side of the Cow Key Bridge. It's the only way on and off the island. Only way to get to the golf course. Put yourself where you can see anyone approaching the bridge in a car or on foot. If you can't take them alive, I would welcome headlines tomorrow about the tragic outcome of an unwitnessed drive-by."

Gorse phoned Fagan. "It's coming together now. He's sending me to Key West to help him finish it. He'll join up later."

Said Fagan, conspiratorially, "You and me. Him. I like the odds."

"He doesn't know exactly where the stocks are hidden but he knows to get to them you have to cross the bridge between Key West and Stock Island. I'm to stand sentry and stop the reporter when he makes his move."

"You take one side of the bridge. I'll take the other."

"And there's a woman, too. She works for Griff. She took off and he thinks she switched sides. I'm to find her, too."

There was no response for a moment, and then Fagan said, "I can help you there. I'm looking at the current location of her car right now."

"I'm impressed," said Gorse. "I'm moving now. Come when you can. I'll let you know where I am."

"No need," replied Fagan. "I'm tracking you, too."

Morning came with rising wind and low dark scudding clouds moving fast. Bands of squalls were already delivering sporadic punishment to the island. Maxine was a compact, fast-moving cyclone and would not linger. Landfall was forecast for the middle Keys by late morning. The sun could yet reappear before dusk.

Milo, Danny and the Eskimo were at a table off the galley. The Eskimo poured coffee. "The Polly is as secure as she can be. She'll be fine. I've triple-checked the fenders and chafing gear. The new pilings are high and the dock will rise with a surge. I'll ride it out on another client's boat. It's small and will see some batting about. I'll have to adjust the lines through the blow. You're on your own till the wind slackens."

Milo said, "We'll be fine. It's just a short drive to the golf club and if we see something the key fits we collect what's inside and we come right back. And if there's nothing there, we come right back."

"And again, I can't thank you enough for your kindness," said Danny.

Mack appeared on the dock. "Permission to come aboard."

Inside he took a coffee and a seat. "The Weather Channel says she is the most obedient storm in years. Since Labor Day it's followed the predicted track almost spot-on. And the millibars are cooperating, too. Unless Maxine's been playing possum her intensity should stay below a three. Right around ninety knots. That goes out twenty-five miles from center. Center will be roundabout Marathon. Between forty and fifty miles from us. So figure roughly sixty knots here tops, with gusts of eighty."

"Sounds like Rita when it passed south," Milo remembered. "Same year as Wilma and Katrina. Pushed a five foot surge across the southernmost point and a dozen cackling assholes danced around the marker buoy taking videos of themselves getting knocked flat by waves bashing the sea wall."

Milo converted knots in his head. "Still and all, seventy mile-an-hour sustained is a walk in the park, all things considered."

Danny was no stranger to hurricanes. "But we should get back here before those ninety mile-an-hour gusts do."

Said Milo to Mack, "Moses is heading out. We should, too."

The rain was coming down and the top was up as Milo drove, with Danny shotgun and Mack hunched in

the rear seat with his legs straddling the hump.
Roosevelt was nearly absent of traffic as they cruised
through a steady rain along the north loop of Roosevelt
Boulevard encircling the east end. In Milo's pocket were
two keys. He thought it improved the odds that one or
the other would fit, though Al had insisted they were
identical. After a few minutes Milo turned onto Route 1,
the approach to the channel bridge and Stock Island in
view beyond it.

"Milo! Stop!" Danny cried in alarm. "That's Gorse.
At the bridge!"

The three spied two men standing on the sidewalks
astride the bridge threshold. One suddenly became
agitated and both reached their arms into their jackets.
There was a single turn lane ahead of the bridge and
Milo wheeled into it, fishtailing on wet pavement as he
completed the U-turn and fled back to the intersection
with Roosevelt. Instead of retracing his route he turned
left and accelerated as best he could around the south
loop of the island. If there was a pursuit, Milo would
lose them on a twisting tangle of back streets on his
return to the marina.

Danny caught her breath. "He's here."

Mack asked, "So was the other guy Cameron?"

"I've seen Cameron," said Milo. "Not him."

Danny turned to face Mack. "I don't know him. Griff
must have brought reinforcements."

"Well, that leaves us dead in the water," said Milo.
"Gotta toss out plan A."

By the time they boarded the Lucky Polly Mack had
devised plan B.

Half an hour had elapsed since they had left the boat, and in that time the anemometer reading on the instrument panel had climbed markedly.

"You're nuts," said Milo.

"You gave me the idea. 'Dead in the water.' The water!"

"But I don't wish to be dead in it."

"Come on, Milo, you and I have ridden together in rough water plenty of times. Okay, maybe Maxine dials that up to eleven. But the skill set is the same."

Mack motioned for Milo and Danny to follow and led the way down stairs and through a corridor abaft to the stern garage of the Lucky Polly. There, Mack pointed to twin PWCs nested in individual deployment cradles. The Polly was berthed with her bow facing the harbor fairway, the dock to starboard. The port side was clear, no neighboring craft, and the garage door on that side of the yacht facilitated the easy launching of watercraft.

Mack turned to Milo. "Okay, so some way, we don't know how, those guys knew we needed to cross that bridge. But think about it. If they knew where we were going beyond the bridge they could have just waited there to jump us. We'll flank them. Power over to Sunset next to the golf course." Milo knew he meant Sunset Marina. "Kawasaki 310s. Big and heavy. Muscle to spare. Top speed seventy miles an hour."

"But that's on flat water. Can they even make way in hurricane headwinds? How can you not be pushed back if your dash registers fifty and the wind is blowing in your face at eighty?"

Forget the wind. The PWC only feels the water. It's aerodynamic and the air speed friction will be minimal.

Your own body will feel the wind but hell, you drive a convertible. Ever stick your head above the windshield going ninety? That's what you'll feel. But with a helmet you'll do fine. It'll shield you from the sting of the spray. Tell yourself you're having fun. Got it?"

"So in heavy waves we'll be throttling up and down like a yoyo. And we can't open it up. So how long do you think from here to Sunset?"

"I'm a dive instructor. I didn't have to take Newtonian mechanics. I know shit about hydrodynamic drag. The drag coefficient depends on the shape of the object moving through the water and how fast it's going. More speed, more friction. But when you drop the hammer on the jet drive, the planing hull lifts the bow above the waves and reduces drag. The surge raises the depth of the water near the shore, and more depth means higher waves. Try to minimize launching off the wave crests and stay as best you can down in the troughs where the jet drive can maintain purchase. You've ridden in heavy weather. Hurricane winds aren't constant and the waves will come from every angle. But you can read them and duck around the crests. You'll be fine. And if you fall off, just don't panic. Grab your tether and pull back aboard and carry on. So to your question, how long will it take for us to get to the marina? I have no fucking idea."

Mack unzipped a large duffel and pulled out black wet suits and neoprene flotation vests. From a bin he lifted two matt-black polycarbonate full-face helmets and a pair of goggles. "When we take off the helmets, the goggles will protect our eyes from the blowing rain. It'd sting like hell."

They suited up. To Danny, they looked like a fusion of Black Panther and space villain. Lastly, Mack took a rain jacket of the same color as the rest of the ensemble from a hook and passed another to Milo. They provided needed pockets; Milo for his phone, the keys and the printed clues. Mack for his service sidearm. He chambered a round and added another to his clip. His M9 was fitted with a laser, which he'd found effective up to a distance of nearly half a football field. He'd put holes in cans at a greater distance with sight alone. Some friends still in service preferred the Sig, but Mack had cashiered out before the Army abandoned the Beretta and, like most, he favored the hardware to which he was most accustomed. A good weapon for operating, like today, behind enemy lines.

Danny said, "You two have lost your minds. Take a breath and think. You could drown on the trip over. You could be murdered when you get there. And you don't know for certain anything is there to find. Nobody gets hurt if you just call police and let them deal with Griff and Gorse."

Milo raised his visor and smiled. "But then the police run the show and we're watching from the cheap seats."

Mack grinned. "No guts, no glory. If there's nothing at the end of the rainbow, we ride back and sic the law on the bad guys. But if we find it…" He said no more. Mack punched the button that opened the garage door. The side of the boat fell away and stopped just below the waterline, creating a ramp. Another switch extended the steel deployment cradles into the water. He showed Danny how to withdraw the cradles and close the door. The two mounted up and moved away, disappearing

from view with a roar as they accelerated into the
channel.

Chapter 22

Outside the seawall Milo followed Mack into the tempest. The waves danced violently around him and driven sheets of spray rat-tatted on his visor. The helmet helped to mute Maxine's howl. For many minutes, he had no way of knowing how many, his thoughts were razor-focused on the same repetitive movements. Standing to avoid the spinal shocks from the relentless impacts on the rock-hard sea, he bent his knees to cushion the blows. At times he sat on the seatback support bolster to give his thighs a break. His throttling up and down was unremitting. He observed that the counterclockwise winds were blowing him on shore, and he turned seaward into the waves. Now weightless flying off a crest, then wham, into the trough, the pounding was ceaseless. But despite close calls he did not capsize, and for the first time he felt they were making real progress when Fleming Key appeared faintly through the gloom.

United States Navy real estate speckles the bottom
Keys like a fragmented moth-eaten quilt. Boca Chica
Key, the east stepping stone beyond Stock Island, is a
sprawl of runways and habitat to jet jockeys. The word
Navy arouses images of fighting ships. But since the
surface ship and submarine base closed in the 1970s,
Naval Air Station Key West is all about planes. A naval
presence in Key West has spanned two centuries, but
because it is Key West it remains an unconventional
presence. The base is owned by the Navy but its use is
ecumenical, as flyboys from the Air Force and Marines
also train there and lift glasses at local bars with visiting
pilots from allied forces. Fighter jets take off and land
above a sandy beach where naturists in their birthday
suits wave in vigorous appreciation of the daily air
show. On Key West the Navy is also landlord of the
Coast Guard base and the Truman Annex is now home
to a multi-agency joint taskforce to detect and foil illicit
smuggling of drugs and contraband. Here, lucky liaison
officers from the UK, France, Spain, the Netherlands,
Canada, Brazil, Mexico and other nations in Central and
South America and the Caribbean happily find
themselves assigned; a two block walk from the bars of
Duval Street.

And the United States Army is permanently camped
out on the far end of Fleming Key, a slender island
property of the Navy base, a stone's throw from the
Coasties. There, Special Forces dive instructors coach
the next generation of American badasses in the skills of
underwater combat. Mack had worked on the island for
twenty years as an instructor and administrator.

Mack and Milo passed beneath the bridge over which Mack had driven to work countless times. The island blocked the worst of the onshore winds and provided a shelter and a brief reprieve to their muscles. Then it was back into the maelstrom. Intermittent blasts of rain had intensified and now spiked in the open ocean at a horizontal intensity of a fire hose. His concentration was broken only by a flitting moment of pure lucidity in which he was suddenly aware beyond doubt that this was absolutely and positively the dumbest thing he had ever been talked into. Milo was glad for the helmet as the shock of impact in the bumpy seas more than once threw his head forward onto the handlebar.

At length they passed beneath the bridge to Navy-owned Dredgers Key, beyond which Stock Island came into view. First Mack, and then Milo turned at last into the protected channel and arrived at Sunset Marina. They tied up swiftly and secured their helmets in the bow lockers. In less than five minutes they were over a short fence and onto the golf course.

Mack said, "This is the eleventh hole on the back nine. We follow it to the green and make our way south from there." He led the way past a cluster of golf-view homes and together they descended the fifteenth fairway to its tee, which Mack said would put them hard by two and three. Palm trees were bowed by the keening wind that whipped up white caps on the water hazards. Chances they'd be spotted by residents watching the storm from their windows were slim; still they crossed to the far side of the course and crept stealthily—jacket hoods up—goggle-eyed ninjas.

In the salon of the Lucky Polly, Danny stood by a window peering out into Maxine's black heart. It wasn't yet noon but the slate-gray clouds had dimmed the sun to the murk of late dusk. Her anxiety had grown as intense as the storm outside with the passage of time. It had been nearly forty minutes. Surely they would have arrived at the marina by now. Were they both lost? She had turned off her phone on her drive down the Keys with the battery nearly dead. She had recharged it overnight in her stateroom and now powered it up and texted. *Milo. Where are you? Are you safe?* There was nothing else to do.

"This is the place, "said Milo, as they neared the green on two. "Straight to the road from here." The number of paces was irrelevant, but Milo counted off three short of the fifty instructed by the verse. Longer legs than the clue-giver, he supposed. After hopping a waist-high fence the final paces placed them on a paved walkway. The Florida Keys Overseas Heritage Trail is a pedestrian pathway linking the Keys along US 1 parallel to the extinct Flagler railroad. There was nothing to the left of them save grass and trees between the fence and the road to where the pathway vanished in the constant rain. Milo knew the road was narrower than the old train bed, and calculated that whatever the hiding place was, it had to be beyond the edge of the ballast; the stone aggregate supporting the sleepers and track. "Heaped stones are the border; steel a footstep too far." In his mind's eye he saw the gravel bed spilling across the path on which he stood. They turned to the right. A half-block distant was the junction with Cross Street. Tall light poles illuminated the pedestrian crossing. A pair of

what Milo imagined were electrical boxes serving the
traffic lights stood side by side along the trail. And
behind them, between the trail and the golf course fence,
was some box-like object on a pedestal. Milo noted that
leafy tree canopy above would have hidden it from
satellite map view. There were zero cars on the road.
They leaned into the wind. A rain band had passed and
visibility had improved. In moments they reached the
object. It was an industrial-looking iron box, at shoulder
height supported by a heavy metal post anchored solidly
in the ground. It gave the appearance of advanced age,
but had been freshly painted in institutional gray and a
descriptive plaque was inscribed on the side facing the
trail. "Vintage railroad trackside telephone box. Installed
at intervals on railways to receive instructions or to
report trouble. Cast iron. Stromberg-Carlson Telephone
Manufacturing Company, Rochester, N.Y. Sales office
Chicago, Ill. Used during construction of the Overseas
Railroad to Key West, Ca. 1908 into the early years of
operation, 1911-1920. Preserved and dedicated as an
artifact of the Florida Keys Overseas Heritage Trail,
August 7, 2004." Milo knew plans for the work-in-
progress Heritage Trail called for educational kiosks and
historical markers along its length from Key West to
Key Largo.

   "Gotta be." Said Mack. "Built like a tank. Padlock
big as the palm of my hand. Look at those hinges. Like a
safe."

   Said Milo, "But would they just paint the thing
without looking inside? Another reason there may not
be a payday."

   "Only one way to find out."

As he reached into his pocket Milo's phone vibrated. He checked it and replied to Danny that they were safe and at the golf course. He returned the phone to his pocket and took out one of his two keys. "Al said this cover over the keyhole is called a drop. You slide it over to insert the key and a spring pulls it back to cover the hole when you remove the key. Keeps dirt and bugs out. But it's stuck. I think it's the paint."

Mack pulled out his pistol and used the grip to tap on the metal. It broke loose. Milo slid the drop clear of the keyhole. He inserted the key and felt it pushing ancient tumblers as he turned it. The shackle popped free. He removed it and dropped it to hang from its chain while he pulled on the brawny handle. The door pulled back smoothly on its hinges and swung more than 180 degrees to fully expose the interior. Inside was a phone.

"It's just a telephone," groaned Milo. On the left side of the open compartment dangled a handset, the size and shape of a standard candlestick phone earpiece of the era. On the right side of the compartment was a panel from which projected a shiny black mouthpiece. There was nothing else.

Mack said, "There was one more verse. A final clue."

Milo pulled out his phone and read the words. "Fortune hinges on hearing. It calls to you clearly."

"Look here at this thing."

Mack had unhooked a small metal crank fastened by a clip beneath the speaking tube. "There's a hole right below in the center of this panel. Some old-timey way to alert the operator? I've seen movies where you crank a phone."

Milo took the hand-crank and inserted it into the hole. "Let's see what happens. No. It's not turning fast like a generator crank. It's is turning like a wind-up music box. Like a mainspring is being tightened." Like an old phonograph, thought Milo. "Fortune hinges on hearing." He grasped the handset and lifted it to his ear, and he withdrew the turning lever to release the tightened spring. The wind was still blowing in a persistent undulating wail, but he could clearly hear a mechanical humming and from the handset came a sound. It began as a hiss, and then a voice spoke to him across a century of time.

Gorse picked up and Cameron said, "Her phone is back on. I'll call you when I have her."

Chapter 23

"The next voice you hear will be that of Thomas Edison, the brilliant man," spoke the baritone voice dripping with self-importance. Each syllable rang with almost comically precise elocution. Milo remembered all the early Edison records were introduced by such an announcer. There was a slight pause and then came the unmistakable reedy tenor voice Milo had heard in newsreels. "Your grit and your wit will be rewarded within. Pull on the cradle from which you took the earpiece you hold in your hand. Behind the door find a satchel. Take it to the offices of J.P. Morgan and Company in New York City. A letter of instruction will be found in the satchel. When you have submitted the certificates you will be delivered by my own train carriage to the Edison Works in New Jersey. Congratulations. I look forward to our visit."

Milo repeated what he had heard to Mack. "Had anyone managed to open the phone box they would not have known there was a compartment behind it. That's what it means. 'Fortune hinges on hearing. It calls to you clearly.'"

Milo grasped the headset cradle and tugged. The hinged panel opened like a door and revealed a compartment behind.

Ch-whang! The bullet impact pealed like a bell as it struck the open iron door. Milo and Mack turned toward the shot muffled by the howl and saw, on the trail from the bridge, distant figures moving in the gloom. In an instant Milo decided and slammed first the inner door and then closed and padlocked the outer door. Carrying the satchel would slow their flight. Mack's gun appeared in his hand and he fired without aiming in the direction of the shadowy figures.

"No way I hit anything, but it'll send a message," said Mack as the running figures ducked behind some indistinct vegetation. In seconds he and Milo had vaulted the fence and sprinted across the golf course. Milo wondered fleetingly how category two hurricane winds might affect the trajectory of a bullet. He decided he did not wish to participate in the experiment. Above the wind, another shot was heard, and another. And Mack went down. Milo crouched beside him. "My thigh. Went through, I think." Mack felt his wetsuit and said, "Two holes. Went through." Milo hoisted him erect and they moved together, Mack with one arm around Milo's neck and the other pointed back toward their pursuers, firing blindly. After several minutes, they paused for breath and saw no sign of movement behind them. Mack assumed the shooters had opted sensibly not to expose themselves to return fire on the open fairways. Blood colored his boot but the tight wetsuit acted to some degree like a tourniquet.

They found their way off the course and into a home development to further lose pursuers. As they passed a house Milo paused. Standing at the end of the drive was a figure of an upright manatee, holding a mailbox. An idea occurred to Milo. It might help to hedge his bets in the increasingly likely event he could not return to retrieve the certificates. He took out one of his pair of keys, placed it in the mailbox, and they moved on. When at last they arrived at the marina they agreed it best to abandon Mack's PWC and together mounted the other. Mack clung to Milo as the dock receded behind them. Milo's phone buzzed in his pocket and the screen displayed Danny. He answered and said, "Mack's been shot. We're on the way. Find a first aid kit." Cameron's voice replied, "I don't believe that will be necessary. You have something of mine. And I have someone who will live only as long as you obey me now." Milo said low to Mack, "Griff has Danny."

"She invalidated our partnership," continued Cameron. "I will trade her for the package." Milo knew Griff would not trade Danny for the package. Nor could he allow anyone with knowledge of the scheme share with authorities the interesting and prosecutable account of how Griff and Gorse acquired their fabulous wealth.

"Okay. You're in charge. But I don't have it. We were ambushed and ran. I left it where it was. But I have the key."

"I'll trade for that. Right now. No delay. Go to Garrison Bight. The Yacht Club. The dock at the Club entrance. Just now Danny and I will have a little chat and I'll bring her along. My man will meet you there. Do what he says. Go directly now. If you are a no-show in twenty minutes I will assume you have foolishly tried something cute and Daniela will die. If we see police Daniela will die. And it would be terribly selfish of you to bother first responders in such weather."

Milo needed to stall. Just for a few minutes. He took a shot. "The storm has moved up and the trailing winds are blasting straight into my face from the west. I'll have to wheel out behind Dredger's Key to block the worst of it. Then it's into the open sea and a rough crosswind crossing to the marina. If I push it, I can make it in a half-hour."

"See you then." Griff disconnected. Milo stopped just inside the breakwater. He called the station. Marty Martin had drawn the short straw to man the fort in the storm. "Marty, listen. Record this call so you don't forget anything. Is it rolling? I have to talk fast and I want you to do everything I say and do it just the way I say it. Don't interrupt. You've got this thing for Savannah Guthrie, right? How'd you like the Today Show to fly you to New York? Answer questions on national TV with waving tourists behind you in the window. Then do this. Repeat what I say on the air right now and you will be a star character in the biggest story there is by tomorrow. Might even get a selfie with Al Roker. Okay, here it is…"

Milo made one more call before throttling into the sea past the breakwater. Conditions on the water had improved somewhat and he managed the transit through the cut without misadventure. He passed Trumbo Point entering Garrison Bight just before the deadline. Power seemed to be out across the Bight. No lights on the docks or outside the shuttered clubhouse. Approaching a

dim and empty Roosevelt Boulevard he made the turn
toward the yacht club docks and saw Gorse and the
unknown man together awaiting them. Both men held
pistols. "Your weapon," Fagan said to Mack. Mack
lifted the Beretta over his head and Gorse leaned in to
collect it. Milo helped leverage Mack onto the dock
beside the club door. Struggling to stand on his bleeding
leg, Mack winced in pain. His face was pallid. "Lucky
shot," he said through clenched teeth. Fagan and Gorse
exchanged words, apparently renewing an argument
over which of them had fired the shot that caused the
wound. Fagan then told Gorse to bind the prisoners with
a bow line lifted from a boat cleat, and to stow them
both in the back of his rental SUV idling within view on
the drive close by. "I'll keep watch for Cameron," he
said. "When his car pulls in, I'll stand in that dark place
by the building. You stay by the car with your gun out.
When he steps out, we both shoot. If he uses the girl as a
shield, shoot them both.

The chilling exchange shook Milo. A new wrinkle. It
hadn't occurred to him the nameless man was not a
Cameron toady, but a foe. Griff would arrive to a
mutiny. And Danny would be in the middle. Mack
groaned as injured thigh muscles spasmed while his
hands were roughly tied. But Griff had already arrived.
Pushing Danny ahead of him, her hands bound and
mouth gagged, he appeared from the corner of the
clubhouse behind Fagan. "Hello Vento," he said
casually. "Dodged a bullet once. Won't happen again."
Fagan wheeled around with his gun arm extended. Gorse
fired twice, striking Fagan in the shoulder and in the
side of his chest. Fagan spun and stumbled, falling onto

the edge of the dock, the momentum tumbling his body into the dark water between two large rocking boats. Gorse returned to binding his captives as Cameron joined them, dragging Danny. A red welt was visible on her cheek, wide eyes staring aghast at where Fagan had vanished. "Very good, Morris. You chose wisely. Your sins are forgiven." Gorse did not reply. He wouldn't bet on his reprieve being irrevocable. He had phoned Cameron immediately after his first meeting with Vento Fagan.

"Put them all in the car," said Cameron. "Give me the man's gun." Griff checked the clip and counted six rounds remaining. Enough. He sat in front as Gorse drove, his gun trained on the trio in the back. Mack slumped between Milo and Danny, delirious from blood loss; his face ashen. The car shook in a sudden gust, but the cyclone's center was forging steadily northward. Sheets of rain were sporadic and no longer blinding. They crossed the bridge to find Stock Island with power. Street lights reflected off the glistening road; theirs the only car in view. "Here," said Milo. Cameron directed Gorse to pull behind a souvenir store off Cross Street so it would not draw attention from a passing cruiser. "Get out. Find your key," Griff ordered. Milo led the way as Cameron, with the gun at his side, followed at a distance.

Milo's mind raced. What could he do? Even had his on-the-fly plan been carried off, Griff would be homicidally enraged. And if it had come to nothing, Griff would have the securities and no incentive to prolong the lives of three nettlesome pains in the ass. As he stood at the iron box he fumbled as he took out the

key, dropping it. Kneeling to retrieve it, he pushed aside
stones at his feet and caught a glimpse of metallic brass.
His second key. He supposed that part of the plan had
been managed. He rose and opened the padlock. The
iron door swung open and Cameron motioned him to
stand aside as he stepped near to examine the interior.
He glowered at Milo, who said, "There's another
compartment behind. Griff stepped back and Milo
pulled the headpiece cradle. The panel opened wide to
reveal…nothing. Milo had rehearsed what he would say,
but had no faith he could sell it. "I figured you needed to
see for yourself. This should convince you. I had time to
move the documents. I stashed them between here and
the yacht club. If you release the others…let Danny get
help for Mack…I give you the stocks.'

Cameron's face contorted with contempt as he curled
his lip and snarled. "You mistake your position. You
have nothing to bargain with. You and your friend
opened the box together. You remained together till this
moment. He knows what you know. Let's take a walk
back to the car and I'll enjoy a chat with him. I imagine
it will be informative. And if not I will simply put
another hole in him. Or her. You choose." Cameron
prodded Milo beneath his shoulder blade with the barrel
of the gun. Milo was out of options. The only choice left
to him was to refuse to choose. This cold-blooded snake
would kill them both anyway. And, after learning that
the stocks were lost to him, would kill Milo, too. Their
footsteps splashed on Route 1 as Maxine unleashed
another gusty deluge to manifest she was still in charge.

Chapter 24

The morning sun blazed in a cloudless sky. Maxine was churning the Gulf two hundred miles off Tampa. She had been promoted to a Cat Three and was taking a bead on Pensacola. She was no longer a topic of conversation at the Schooner Wharf Bar.

Millie Mae said, "So the cops were there?"

Cal sipped his Lime Rickey and grimaced, appreciatively. Millie had been generous with the gin. "They were waiting at the car."

Junie returned from delivering drinks to the far end of the bar.

"What'd I miss?"

"Start over," said Millie Mae.

The Eskimo shielded his eyes from the sun as he perceived a familiar figure striding toward them on the boardwalk.

"Let's get it from the horse's mouth."

The Eskimo had earlier retrieved his employer's watercraft, pleased to find that Maxine had thoughtfully washed away Mack's blood.

Jack Matthews took a seat beside Cal and turned to include Ben and the Eskimo.

"You were last on my witness interview checklist."

Cal nodded and smiled. "The Don is driving. He'll hike over later if you stick around. I'll buy you a drink if you can rehash an abbreviated synopsis for Junie. She's craving details of the sum and substance of how it all went down."

"Booker's and water." All waited until the detective sergeant had a taste.

"First," said Jack, "How's Mack?"

"He's good," replied Ben. "A little fresh blood does wonders. He told me they'll probably let him go tomorrow. He'll be a gimp for a month but you know Mack. In a couple of days he'll be back here showing off his battle scars."

"What happened after Milo called you?" Cal prompted.

"First he called the station. Radio, not police station. He told the on-air guy to put out a message that was especially for anybody living on the golf course. The message was that there was a key hidden in a mailbox shaped like a manatee at a house near the second hole. He said whoever found that key and hustled over to the antique railroad call box along US 1 opposite the T-shirt store on Cross Street should open it. That whoever got there with the key would find a fortune. And as everybody knows that lady in the golf course community happened to be listening. She always had the radio on when she was painting faces on coconuts. Sells them at art fairs." The detective savored another sip.

Junie lifted her phone, "This is on the newspaper Twitter feed. 'Amanda King of Golf Club Drive, 42, told the Citizen she owned the mailbox that was held by a figure of an upright manatee (see photo). She enjoys dressing it in seasonal holiday costumes through the year. Despite the tropical storm-force gusts and rain she ran outside and found the key. On foot she crossed the golf course behind her home to arrive at the large metal railroad communications box along the historical trail adjacent to the Overseas Highway. She opened the padlock just as police arrived. She withdrew the large leather tote bag from the box and officers took the key from her as they hurried her to their mobile command truck concealed a block away. She described it as a very comfortable RV and said she was excited to have been given a tour by officers.'"

Ben said, "Did you see her on the early news? She said when she found out about what Milo and Mack did she was so grateful to them that she plans to give them each a finder's fee of a million each. Chump change to her. Figure the IRS will skim 370,000, they get 630 grand. No Florida income tax. Sweet."

Cal cautioned, "That's if she collects. The SEC is looking into it."

Ben said, "Knock on wood. Mack and Milo say if it happens they'll throw the rest of us a bone. He winked, "Enough to cover enough bar tabs to drink ourselves to death and pay funeral expenses."

Cal grinned, "Hey Ben. Fifty bucks from my share if you help defend my cut from the tax man."

Matthews resumed. "Anyhow, Milo's second call was to me. He explained the situation and said he knew protocol was that cops don't respond to 911 calls in winds above forty-five miles an hour. It was gusting more than twenty miles an hour above that. He then ticked off some compelling mitigating circumstances he hoped would result in an exception to the rule. He said he would stall to afford me time to organize. And then he told me where, if he was going to be murdered, his body would likely be found. He knew it was a straight shot from police HQ to Stock Island, and told me if we saw anybody opening the roadside call box we should escort that person to safety, lock the box and place the key beneath the gravel on the ground. I found a stone that pretty much covered it up. He told us to watch for a car that would likely be the only one on the road leading out of town, and to surprise its occupants only after spotting Milo exiting the car and approaching the phone box. Then we should just do what cops do to stop people from getting shot dead. So we did."

Junie hopped and clapped. "And you're a hero!"

Jack grinned and said, "Does that improve my chances?"

"Why officer. I hope you brought your cuffs," Junie grinned back.

Said Millie Mae, "What about the bad guys?"

"So you must have read the part where the guy who was shot at the Yacht Club survived. A guy was riding out the storm babysitting his boat when he heard gunshots. He was scared and peeked out and saw figures on the dock and when they drove away he came out to find this Fagan dude bobbing in the water. Fished him out. Fagan's a rat, but now he's officially the rat for the prosecution. Fingered Gorse for a murder in New York.

Gorse also did the museum. Both Gorse and Fagan share credit for putting a bullet through Mack. Danny turned over stolen cylinders and Coral Gables cops found the rest where she said they'd be. And Gorse is spilling all he knows about taking orders from Cameron. Also has evidence of an old killing Cameron did himself."

"And where's Milo?" asked Cal. "My calls go into voice mail."

"He and I spent some time hashing out where the girl fits. She worries the State Attorney sees her as an accomplice. But I was there at the capture and in my version of the story she's a hostage. And she gave prosecutors the gift of exhibit A—the stolen cylinders. A judge should smile on that. But since I couldn't guarantee immunity, Milo said they'd both be making themselves scarce for a while."

"Do you know where they are?" asked Junie.

Jack looked out to the busy marina and thought before answering. "You know how the cop always tells the suspects not to leave town and to surrender their passports? Well…I didn't tell them that."

Cal interjected, "And the saloon grapevine has it you're getting bumped to Division Commander."

Matthews rapped a knuckle on the bar and said, "As it may be or not. But this is Key West so I wouldn't presume to start counting chickens. Now I have questions for you. After one more Booker's."

The Cuban coastline rose from the sea and Milo lifted his binocs to detect a landmark. The Gulf Stream had surrendered its influence on his course and he had shifted his attention from the nav screen. The towers of Hotel Nacional came into focus and he adjusted his course west. Marina Hemingway remained open to visiting American boaters. His pouch containing authorization papers lay in easy reach. Journalistic activity was unrestricted by both governments and his global notoriety as a news celebrity had greased the wheels for an approving nod from the Department of State. Danny was technically traveling as his producer but would have qualified under the family visit or professional research license. Their destination was the beach town of Playa Jibacoa, an hour's drive from the marina east along the coast. Danny had family there who were delighted to host her. But first, a few days together in Havana.

She had come into his bed two nights before, following their rescue and hours of police questioning. They were bone-tired and moved slowly; friendly-like. They slept deeply. In the morning they had resumed their exploration, hungrily and with reciprocal initiative. She was sleeping now in the v-berth of the cuddy. He looked down again to peek past the galley at the smudged bottoms of her bare feet and her nut-brown knees curled into her breasts.

He liked the boat. It was nimble and the configuration of the hull made for a cushy ride, even in today's chop. He'd borrowed it for a test drive from a friend whose home repair bills after Irma made him a motivated seller. A Holby Pilot 24, custom built in Bristol, Rhode Island. Recently restored and tricked out. Asking eighty thousand but it was thirteen years old and he knew he could get it for fifty. True, the sleeping cabin had sufficient headroom to allow him to stand only if his legs were amputated above the knee. But his windfall after taxes would cover the boat and fuel and dockage expenses till shrimps learned to whistle. He'd decided to pay off Danny's student loans. Her ordeal, he thought, had earned her a portion of the reward. With no debt she could leave him in her rear-view mirror to dive on Spanish wrecks like some Orange Blossom Lara Croft, but he had no claim on her. Time for the caged bird to fly. Her plans for days ahead included showing him a cave-like habitation in a forested river valley in eastern Cuba with a rocky protrusion providing protection from the elements. Here, humans fashioned tools from stones and pendants from shells more than six thousand years ago. Before, she said, the Mesopotamians invented the wheel. Of course she would know that. A Madrid University team excavating in the region had posted a position for a Spanish-speaker with experience surveying with a magnetometer. Would she and Milo fit together? Would her name get painted on the hull of his boat? He remembered someone said the future is inevitable but invisible. But about the boat name, one thing he knew for sure. The current one had to go. Reef-a-Roni. How about a tip of the hat to TAE? Without the Edison prize there would be no boat. Hmm. Blue Amberol. Not bad. Blue Amberjack? No. He returned his mind to the approaching coast and throttled up.

Epilogue

Marty Martin did not meet Savannah Guthrie. NBC sent Willie Geist to Key West. He conducted the interview at Conch Republic Seafood Company. They sat together at barstools nearest the boardwalk so the background would include the boats decorating the harbor. There had been no selfie with Al Roker. But the chowder was good. And Willie picked up the check.

An army of attorneys from the Securities and Exchange Commissioner and the State Comptrollers of New York and New Jersey almost immediately identified a dozen legal nitpicks that could hold up disbursement of the fortune by the courts for years. The holder of the stocks was not in compliance with almost ninety years of regulations enacted since the Securities Act of 1933, which itself had been enacted four years after the stocks were hidden away. The bearer shares also predated the requirement that a Social Security number be an element of identification of stock ownership. Social Security itself was not born till 1935. Finally, after a surprisingly speedy top-level huddle, it was decided that no harm had been suffered by either the SEC or the states by the glacially protracted process of transfer of ownership. And, truth be told, the lawyers were themselves caught up in the public excitement over the dramatic news accounts of the story. And so the final pronouncement of the establishment bureaucrats was— finders keepers.

The subsequent worldwide response to the story of the Edison contest produced two interesting developments. A Connecticut court clerk who had inherited an Edison player read of the elusive blue amberol cylinder and brought up from the basement the crate of records that had come with the Amberola machine. He spent a portion of a weekend enjoying the music of the Sousa Band, Ada Jones, Edward Meeker and the exuberant harmonies of Collins and Harlan. Then he was struck dumb at the voice of Thomas Edison reading the now-famous verses across the space and time of four generations. How that unlabeled record had come to his family remains unexplained. He recorded a video of the spinning cylinder as it played and posted it on his YouTube channel. Before the end of the day it had racked up fifteen million views.

Secondarily, his discovery, coming as it did after Milo's Edison experts were interviewed by assorted talking heads for days, caused buyers to snatch up every Edison player and cylinder offered for sale on eBay and antique record enthusiast web sites. And downloads of digitized cylinder recordings were the number one trending web searches for a week. Edison's promotion, at long last, accomplished its mission of returning the Edison Records brand to number one in public awareness, at least for a news cycle.

About the Author

Dave McBride is a writer of long acquaintance with the excellent bars of Key West. For more than twenty years he wrote and performed radio humor essays daily for the amusement of Chicago radio listeners. Dave is a winner of an Edward R. Murrow Award for Best Large Market Writing for Radio, and the Best Radio Writing World Gold Medal by the New York Festivals International media awards. After decades of work as a broadcast journalist Dave has traded frigid Midwest Februarys in the big city for the Gulf Stream breezes rustling through the palms in sub-tropical South Florida.

For more of his work visit davemcbride.com.

Acknowledgments

The author wishes to acknowledge the assistance of South Florida University library professionals who helped me navigate the historical stock prices data contained in the Mergent archive database. At Florida Atlantic University's S. E. Wimberly Library, I'm obliged to the Frankels—Ann Frankel, Assistant Serials Coordinator, Collection Management Department, and Ken Frankel, the head of Instruction and Engagement Services who dug up corporate financial reports for Edison companies from the 1931 Moody's Analyses of Investments.

Appreciation, too, for the kind assistance of Sarah Hammill, the Business and Online Learning Librarian at Florida International University, for providing info on public access to the Green Library for purposes of historical stock data research.

And thanks to the President of Adams and Westlake, LTD, Mike Rzeszutko, for granting permission for the use of the image of the company's replica 1912 Adlake #48 railroad switch lock which appears on the cover of this book.

(continued next page)

The Old Custom House in Key West is a town treasure and center of art and history, with ever-changing exhibitions and entertaining events. Nobody gets murdered there. The author loves to visit there.

The Edison/Ford Winter Estates in Fort Myers is a national treasure. 20 scenic acres fronting the Caloosahatchee River showcasing the meticulously preserved home and laboratory where Thomas Edison would feel perfectly at home today. He would certainly enjoy the addition of the visitor's center, exhibiting artifacts from his life and work and a large collection of phonographs representing the years from his invention of recorded sound to Edison's abandonment of the record division. Estate administrators would never have fallen for a scam artist like Griff Cameron. The author loves to visit there.

Made in the USA
Coppell, TX
02 December 2022

87588148R00127